THE POSTBOX MURDERS

Chief Inspector James Holbrooke and the police are utterly baffled by the terrifying activities of the Postbox Killer, an apparent madman who is butchering his victims and stuffing them into village postboxes. It is left to eccentric private investigator Richard Montrose to uncover the killer — and the astonishing reason for his grisly actions . . . While in *Death After Death*, a man is plagued by nightmares and bodily horrors that disappear as inexplicably as they appear. Is he going mad? Or is there another, more macabre explanation?

EDMUND GLASBY

THE POSTBOX MURDERS

Complete and Unabridged

LINFORD
Leicester

First published in Great Britain

First Linford Edition
published 2016

A catalogue record for this book is available
from the British Library.

ISBN 978–1–4448–2771–2

Published by
F. A. Thorpe (Publishing)
Anstey, Leicestershire

Set by Words & Graphics Ltd.
Anstey, Leicestershire
Printed and bound in Great Britain by
T. J. International Ltd., Padstow, Cornwall

This book is printed on acid-free paper

Contents

The Postbox Murders

1

At eighty-seven, Betty Horfield was the oldest resident of the rural south Oxfordshire village of Long Gallop; and yet, despite her age, she was one of the most active. Most mornings, come rain or shine, she managed to get in at least twenty minutes of gardening; and with the size of her front lawn and the wide array of flower beds, not to mention the numerous hanging baskets which adorned her picturesque cottage, it was a task that kept her busy. In the colder months she occasionally hired Pinky Whelps — the handyman, gardener and refuse collector who lived in a caravan on the other side of the river — to help out, but on this fine spring morning she was more than happy to do the work herself.

'Good morning, Betty,' greeted Elsie Paterson, leaning over the garden wall. Four years younger than Betty, she was the second oldest in the village.

Betty looked up at her lifelong friend. She was on her kneeling pad, trowel held tightly, a bucket filled with freshly pulled-up weeds nearby. 'Ah, good morning. Lovely day again,' she commented, wiping the dirt from her hands with an old rag.

Resting a knobbly hand on the garden gate, Elsie paused for a moment, admiring her friend's garden. It truly was spectacular: a blaze of colour and the scent from the roses was most pleasing. 'Yes. The forecast is good for the rest of the day. I plan on getting the bus into town and I was just wondering if there was anything you wanted me to get.'

'Why, that's very kind of you. Let's have a think.' Betty thought for a moment. 'I'm short of tea bags. You know the kind I like; the sort you can't get at the shop . . . and a small brown loaf.'

'Tea bags and a small brown loaf.'

'Yes, that should do me until I get my big shop in on Saturday.' Arthritically and with the aid of her walking stick, Betty got to her feet, her joints creaking audibly. It was not so much the getting down as the getting up that hurt, although on bad days both were equally painful. 'If you hang on a moment I'll accompany you to the post office. I've a few letters I want to send.'

'My bus isn't due for another twenty minutes, so as long as you don't take too long.'

'I won't.' Betty entered her house and came back a short time later holding a handful of letters. 'April's always a busy month when it comes to birthdays,' she told her friend. 'I've got three cards for Wiltshire, two for Wales, one for Scotland and one for America.'

'Are these all relatives?' Elsie asked, holding the garden gate open.

'Mostly. The one to America is for a good friend of mine, Harry Quimby. You remember him, don't you?'

'Oh, of course. How is Harry?'

'Suffering a bit with his lumbago but well otherwise. It'll be his ninetieth soon.'

'Good Lord! I wouldn't have thought him a day over eighty!' With a helping hand, Elsie steered her friend on to the pavement. 'I imagine sending a letter

5

there's quite expensive.'

'Very. It's a good job I only do it twice a year — birthday and Christmas. I couldn't afford it otherwise.' This was a blatant lie, for it was well known in the village that Betty was comfortably well off. She had no living siblings and had never married; consequently she had no dependents, and the money she had inherited from her parents could have bought a street in a much less well-to-do area.

Together the two old ladies set off down the quiet road heading for the post office.

In addition to having a reasonable bus service, Long Gallop was fortunate enough to have not only a post office, but a small doctor's surgery, a church, a primary school and two public houses — the Red Lion and the Fox and Hounds — one on either side of the bridge.

'I hear that there are plans afoot to turn the Red Lion into one of those new wine bars,' commented Elsie as they neared the thatch-roofed inn. 'Such a shame that would be.'

'I wouldn't go believing all that you hear,' replied Betty. 'They've been saying for years that it's going to change hands, but it never has.' A devout teetotaller, she had never once set foot inside, despite her long years in the village. 'And as to it becoming a wine bar, well, they'll be quite a few in the village who'll say no to that. Myself, for one.'

'Did you know that old Andy Westbrooks has left the village?'

Betty was stunned. This was indeed news. 'Andy? Left?'

'Apparently. Nancy Bothwell told me yesterday that he's moved to Yorkshire to live closer to his grandchildren. He wasn't in the best of health, you know. According to Mrs. Johnson at the surgery he was having trouble with his insides. He'd been to the hospital for a lot of tests.'

'Too much drink I suspect,' commented Betty. 'He always was one for the bottle. Come to think of it, I haven't seen him since he got drunk on Ted Humphries's homemade cider at the Queen's Silver Jubilee celebrations last year.'

'That was a lovely day, wasn't it?' Elsie

said enthusiastically. Like most of her generation she was an ardent royalist.

Their progress was slow and doddery but they were now nearing the post office.

It had just gone eight o'clock and it suddenly dawned on Betty that she would not be able to post her letter to America until the post office counter opened at nine. The shop which it was annexed to had been open for several hours, selling papers, sweets, snacks and other bits and pieces.

'I'm going to catch my bus,' said Elsie. 'Have a nice morning, and I'll try and pop round for a chat later in the afternoon.' She turned and headed for the bus stop about hundred yards on the other side of the road.

'Don't forget my tea bags . . . and the bread.'

Elsie turned. 'Don't worry. I won't forget.'

Betty watched her friend hobble down the road. She then headed for the post office, her letters grasped tightly in her hand. Her intention was to post the ones to the UK mainland and return later on in the morning to mail the card to America. She checked that all had first-class stamps on them and the proper addresses, then prepared to slip them through the slot of the black-based red pillar box.

The first envelope met with some resistance and bent slightly before disappearing inside.

Betty paused for a moment. She had never known the pillar box to become so full — not even at Christmas time when the sheer volume of mail sent went up tenfold. She inserted her second envelope and once again had to push harder than expected to get the letter in.

It was then that a foul stink hit her nostrils. At first she thought it was due to the fertiliser that had been sprayed on the surrounding fields, or perhaps even the landfill site two miles away. God alone knew how bad that could be when the wind blew in the wrong direction. This stink, however, seemed to be coming from somewhere much closer at hand, and for a moment her mind entertained the idea that some prankster — perhaps one of the teenage Bentley twins — had put something unpleasant, such as dog excrement, inside the pillar box. It would be the kind of thing those two rascals would get up to.

Suddenly the post office door opened and Gary Thompson, the postmaster, stepped out. He saw Betty and waved. 'Morning, Miss Horfield. Another fine day.' He was about to make another comment when he too detected the unappealing reek.

'I think there's something in your postbox.' Nose wrinkling in disgust, Betty stepped away, her five un-posted letters in her hand.

Thompson cursed under his breath. Moving forward, he noticed that the hatch appeared to have been wrenched open and then hastily closed. He bent down to investigate, opening the metal door.

Along with several blood-spattered letters, a naked, severed arm tumbled out and landed on the pavement.

Thompson leapt back in horrified surprise.

Betty screamed.

Regaining some level of composure, Thompson stared down at the bloody arm and then unwillingly raised his eyes, dreading what he might see.

A largely dismembered corpse had been crammed inside the pillar box.

Both legs had been lopped off and were now wedged tightly inside the metal container, one on either side of the mutilated torso. Mercifully, the head was turned so that he could not discern its features; but from the jet-black mop of unruly hair he had a fair suspicion as to who the unfortunate was — Pinky Whelps.

* * *

Less than an hour later, Detective Chief Inspector James Holbrooke watched and waited as two of his forensic team extricated the grisly body parts from the pillar box and put them in a black body bag. Dozens of photographs had been taken and everything in the vicinity that looked important had been dusted for fingerprints.

A tape barrier and a screen had been erected to ensure that the crowd of interested villagers were kept away and that they did not see the proceedings. News had spread like wildfire throughout Long Gallop, and whilst the details were as yet known to but a handful there were many keen to see what was going on. Nothing like this had ever happened here, at least not in living memory. That this was serious everyone could tell, for there were three police cars and an ambulance parked nearby.

Hugh Caldwell, the village's richest man and lead gossip, had come up with the idea that there had been a bungled raid on the post office and that Gary Thompson had shot dead the burglars. Even Father Frank Jericho from the village church was on the scene, trying his best to reassure people.

Stan Orton, the lead forensic scientist, walked over to where Holbrooke stood, his face grim.

'Well this is a new one,' said Holbrooke. 'Gives a completely new meaning to the phrase 'it's in the post'.'

Orton contained a wry chuckle. After fifteen years serving together he was used to the other's macabre sense of humour.

'So apart from the obvious, anything you can tell me?' Holbrooke asked him.

'Well it would appear that the victim was this Mr. Whelps that Mr. Thompson named. The limbs have been severed somewhat brutally; heavy blows from a cleaver or some other bladed weapon. There's also an impact trauma to the back of the head, which I would guess was the primary wound. Probably caused by a hammer.'

'So you think he was knocked out first?'

Orton nodded. 'It would appear so. Obviously a full post-mortem will tell me more, but at this initial stage I'd say he was cracked over the back of the head, knocked out, taken elsewhere, stripped, dismembered, and placed in here.'

'A very strange place to hide a body, wouldn't you say?'

'I don't think 'hide' is the right word. After all, whoever did this must've known that the postman would collect the mail in the morning.'

'And I don't suppose he had the right postage either.' It was a disrespectful thing to say, but having seen so much death over the years Holbrooke had become inured to it. His making light of a situation others would have undoubtedly considered truly ghastly was his coping strategy; his means of dealing with things like this which he encountered on a regular basis. Only the day before yesterday he had been called out to an incident which had involved a man committing suicide by blowing his brains out with a shotgun. How he had eaten his spaghetti bolognese for supper that evening was anyone's guess.

'There are no stamps on the body if that's what you mean,' answered Orton dryly. 'From the few blood spatters on the pavement I think it's fair to assume that the body was transferred in a sheet of some kind.'

'I imagine the body was placed here sometime during the night.' Holbrooke took in his surroundings. The place was hardly a thriving hub of activity, but surely no one in their right mind would contemplate something as outrageous during daylight hours. Then again, surely no one in their right mind would consider committing such a heinous act in the first place. It seemed clear to him that this had to be the act of a psychopath; a severely deranged individual — surely only someone truly unhinged would ever dream of something as bizarre as this.

'I would guess so,' answered Orton.

'I notice that the wire cage has been removed.'

'What?'

'There should be a mesh cage behind the door to keep the letters in. It's gone. No doubt it was removed in order to get the body in. Whatever sick bastard committed this did so in order to achieve maximum shock value, unless it was someone with a severe grudge against the postal service.' Holbrooke could see that things were coming to a close in regard to the retrieval of the victim.

To his dismay, he noticed that one or two of the local reporters had now turned up on the scene and were in persistent conversation with some of the villagers and one of his constables. There was no disputing the fact that it was going to be extremely difficult to keep something like this under wraps.

The remains of Pinky Whelps were bagged and transported to the waiting ambulance.

Holbrooke's inspector — a fat, balding man named Tyrone Jackson — came out of the post office, where he had been taking down details from the two who had discovered the dismembered corpse. Whilst carrying out his duties he had found time to buy a sausage roll and took a huge bite out of it. Brushing the pastry crumbs from his suit, he strode over to his boss. 'Sir, there's not much to go on, but Mr. Thompson does think that he heard a vehicle outside some time during the night. He's not entirely sure but would guess it to be around three o'clock.' He finished the last of his snack.

'And what of Mr. Phelps's last movements?' Holbrooke asked.

'I've got two officers over at the caravan park at this moment. Apparently he was a bit of a drifter. Did a bit of odd-jobbing throughout the area.'

'Any known enemies?'

'No. Seems he was quite well liked. From all accounts he kept himself to himself. We've had no success in tracking down any next of kin.'

'Hmm.' Holbrooke nodded. 'Well, I don't think there's much more to do here. Try and get as many statements as you can but be sure not to give too much away in terms of the details. I think we'd better hold off making this public for as long as we can, although I've no doubt that the press will get wind of it very soon. Right, I'm going back to the station.'

★　★　★

By eleven o'clock news of the gruesome murder was the main article on all the local radio stations, and by midday it was featured on national television. Over a dozen news reporters converged on Long Gallop. In the hourly broadcasts which followed, the reporters were filmed interviewing many of the villagers, each of whom had their own take on the murder. Inspector Tyrone Jackson was there in his official capacity, fielding questions and doing his best to reassure the public that they were treating this as an isolated and exceptionally rare incident.

It was the four o'clock news bulletin that caught the attention of forty-three-year-old horologist and independent crime investigator Richard Montrose.

Long Gallop was less than a ten-minute drive from where he lived; and as he went to his television and turned up the volume, he saw pictures of the rural village he had driven through on more than a few occasions. He watched, intrigued, as the pretty female news reporter covered the terrible murder, listening attentively to her every word. Once it was over he got up, went over to his cluttered desk and jotted down the salient points on a pad.

For him, investigating unusual murders had become an obsession. It was an unhealthy and at times ghoulish hobby that went way beyond the morbid curiosity of the general public.

He was only too well aware that people who murdered came in every size and shape, from every walk of life, from every age and culture. The insights they offered into human nature fascinated him; knowing that no one, certainly not the criminal psychologists whom he had come to loathe, could ever truly explain just why killers did the terrible things that they did.

There had been nothing like this for a long time. A dismembered body found in a pillar box. As far as he was concerned, it was like a dream come true — for therein lay a mystery to be sure. He would start his investigations by making some inquiries in the village. He had plenty of fake yet genuine-looking badges and methods of identification that would enable him to 'sniff around' without drawing too much attention.

★　★　★

It had just gone six o'clock when Montrose parked his vehicle in the car park of the Fox and Hounds public

19

house. He had seen with his own eyes the infamous pillar box and was now planning on questioning some of the locals. In his mind he had gone over the numerous possible approaches open to him — well aware that to draw too much attention could well be viewed as highly suspicious amongst Long Gallop's inhabitants. He got out and locked up. Now that dusk was approaching, the temperature had dropped considerably; and although it was a fine evening there was a certain coldness in the air, prompting him to put on his coat.

Upon entering, he was somewhat surprised as to just how busy it was. There were a dozen or so around the bar area whilst others were seated at tables partaking of their evening meals. It appeared that, despite the dreadful discovery of this morning, life went on regardless in Long Gallop.

Montrose waited to be served at the bar, ordering a pint of beer which he took over to a table near the door. Briefly he consulted the menu, contemplating whether to have supper here or not. The food on offer looked tempting, and after a minute's deliberation he went back to the bar, pint in hand, and ordered himself a beef pie with mash and peas.

The barman took his money and made a note of his order.

'That was pretty grim what happened here this morning, wasn't it?' Montrose said, his elbows resting on the bar.

The barman shook his head. 'Dreadful. Absolutely dreadful. I knew the victim. Poor bugger used to come in here two or three nights a week. Nice man.'

'My condolences.' Montrose took a sip of beer. 'I don't understand what kind of monster would do such a thing. It's beyond evil if you ask me.'

'I couldn't agree more with you. Now if you'll excuse me . . . ' The barman went to serve another customer. After a few minutes he returned.

'I've lived in Long Gallop for over thirty years and I've never known anything like it,' continued the barman. 'The police have tried to assure everyone that there's nothing to be unduly worried about; but come on, who's going to rest easily in their beds tonight knowing that there's a maniac on the loose? Why, everyone's been advised to go home in pairs, and I know I'll be going to bed with a baseball bat under my pillow.'

'I didn't realise things had got so — '

'Evening, Ken. A pint of your finest and a double whisky when you're ready,' called out a stocky gentleman in a loud, plummy voice. He was dressed in a Barbour jacket, a cloth cap and checked trousers, and he shouldered his way to the bar with a certain arrogance as though he owned the place.

Montrose threw the man an unfriendly glance. From his attire and mannerisms he was without doubt one of the landed gentry. All he was missing was a shotgun cradled under one arm and a brace of dead pheasants in his hand.

'Coming right up, Mr. Caldwell,' said the barman. He busied himself pouring the drinks.

'What a day this has been,' commented the newcomer. 'If I live to be a hundred I doubt whether I'll forget it.'

'I assume you're referring to the

murder?' Montrose asked.

'Indeed I am. A terrible business.' The man extended his hand. 'Hugh Caldwell.'

Montrose returned the gesture. 'Ray Smith. I work for The Oxford Investigator,' he said, using one of his many pseudonyms and fictitious employers. He pulled a wallet from a coat pocket and whisked out a card which he flashed briefly before the other's eyes. 'I take it you're a local?'

'That I am. Born and bred here. And I can tell you something — this was not, I repeat not, done by anyone from Long Gallop.' There was a flicker in Caldwell's eyes. This was something about which he was clearly adamant.

The barman, who was listening in to the conversation, was not convinced. He shook his head. 'I don't know about that, Mr. Caldwell. I think there's a lot more goes on in this village than anyone really knows about.'

'Nonsense,' snorted Caldwell. 'I know nearly everyone in the village.'

'Yeah, nearly everyone. But it's those you don't know that are the ones you've got to look out for. Take those people who live down by where the old garages used to be. They're a weird bunch if you ask me.'

'The Darwins?'

'No, they're all right. It's their neighbours I'm on about. I don't know their names, but you always see him wearing that dark suit and he's always on the move, come day or night.'

'I think he's a doctor in London,' Caldwell responded. 'I've seen him cycling to Baxholme to get the train.'

'Doctor, my arse! There's something downright odd about him if you ask me.'

'I'm sure the police will get round to questioning everyone they suspect of involvement,' said Montrose. He turned to face Caldwell. 'I'm about to have some supper. 'I don't suppose you'd care to join me?'

'I've already eaten but I'll gladly sit at your table,' Caldwell answered.

When they had taken their places, Montrose began the conversation by asking: 'Do you have any ideas as to who might have done this, and why?'

'None whatsoever. It's a complete mystery.' Caldwell finished his whisky. 'As you can no doubt imagine there are all sorts of colourful rumours flying around the village, and some are already levelling blame at those they don't get on with. It's like how it was in medieval times when the peasants accused their neighbours of witchcraft. I suppose people are becoming paranoid. But I'm positive that this was done by a stranger.'

'Anything you can tell me about the victim?'

'Pinky? There isn't much to tell. He used to spend his days doing odd jobs around the village. A bit of painting and decorating or some gardening for some of the older villagers. Salt of the earth. Nobody ever had a bad word to say about him. Sometimes he'd go away and we wouldn't see him for weeks. God alone knows where he went.'

Montrose turned his attention to the main door, aware that a huge broad-shouldered man with a massive grey beard had stomped into the public house, his eyes wide and staring.

'Evening, Badger,' the barman cried, raising a hand in greeting.

'Bloody hell!' the bearded man rumbled, his voice gravelly. 'Have you heard the latest? They've found another one over in Thelford. Same thing — a butchered body inside a postbox! Bloody world's gone mad, I say.' He turned to the barman and bellowed for a beer.

2

Second Body Discovered in Postbox!

Late yesterday afternoon a second severely mutilated naked body was found crammed into the postbox at Thelford, south Oxfordshire, less than ten miles from where the first gruesome find was made. The remains of the first victim, who has been named locally as Mr. Peter 'Pinky' Whelps, were discovered by a member of the public. Police have not as yet disclosed the identity of the second victim; however there are fears that a serial killer is at large, and Detective Chief Inspector James Holbrooke of Thames Valley Police has asked all members of the public to be extra vigilant and to report anything suspicious to their local police station immediately.

★　★　★

Montrose read the newspaper article a second time before pouring out his coffee and beginning on his breakfast of kippers and toast. He lived alone in a nondescript two-bedroom house in a small cul-de-sac; and despite having been there for nigh on fifteen years, he could not recall having ever spoken with his neighbours. It was not as though he was antisocial; it was just that their paths never really crossed, and he felt he had very little in common with them anyway.

Yet, in truth, it was not he who avoided those nearest to him but they who avoided him. For he was seen by others, particularly those with a more judgemental slant, as a bit of an oddball; a recluse who lived a rather secretive life. Which, as far as he was concerned, was all to the good. It enabled him to get on with what he enjoyed doing and, as of yesterday, something with real potential had come his way. As he sat there, finishing off the last of his breakfast, he was already trying to put himself into the mind of the killer, wondering just what kind of being could and, more to the point, would, do something like this.

He was eager to go and see for himself the location where the latest victim had been discovered, but he was only too well aware that he had several clocks awaiting repair. One of them was a stunningly ornate Winterhalder and Hofmeier Ting Tang walnut-cased bracket clock, which just needed a final inspection and polish before he could contact its owner and inform him it was finished. There was still a fair amount of work to do on some of the other clocks, but he hoped to have it all done by lunch-time.

★   ★   ★

'So, who have we got here, then?' inquired Detective Chief Inspector Holbrooke as Orton and his assistant removed the un-shapely black bag from the cold storage morgue locker.

'We believe this individual to be Mr. Jason Bennet.' The forensic scientist offloaded the bag onto an operating table. With a snap, he put on his surgical gloves and then opened the plastic sack.

Holbrooke grimaced and instinctively brought a hand to his mouth. After all, it was not pretty. For some reason he was reminded of a scene from Jaws. It was hard, even for him with all of his experience of dead bodies, to believe that this person had been killed by another human being and not a monstrous great white shark. 'And . . . he's the one that was found in Thelford yesterday evening?

'Yes.'

'Any noticeable differences from Mr. Whelps?'

'Nothing.' Orton removed a naked arm that had been severed just below the shoulder. 'As you can see, the method of removal was fairly crude. The marks on the flesh and bone would indicate a vicious downward hacking. It would require a fair amount of strength to chop through the bone. Similarly with the legs.'

'Would something like a cleaver fit the bill?'

'Cleaver . . . axe. A heavy-bladed weapon.' Orton unwrapped the head and torso from the bag. He smoothed back a patch of lank brown hair to reveal a bloodied imprint on the side of the skull.

'Exactly the same. A concussive blow to the back of the head.' Holbrooke sighed, his fears that there was a serial killer at large now confirmed. 'We're going to have to establish whether there's any connection between the victims, but I've a gut feeling that the killer's an opportunist.'

'There's two connections so far: sex and morphology,' noted Orton. 'Both victims were men and both were fairly slim, certainly under eleven stone. Height-wise, I think we're looking at five-six, five-seven at most. Any larger and I think the killer would have struggled getting them inside the postboxes. So as long as you stick to the canteen pies, James, you'll be safe.'

★ ★ ★

Montrose had listened attentively to the news updates on his small radio as he had stripped down and repaired one of his clocks. He had converted his spare bedroom into a small workshop, and it was here that he also kept his fairly large collection of crime books, all detailing the lives and deaths of various notorious murderers.

The latest bulletins added nothing new to the story, but he did sense a growing alarm within the wider community, demonstrable in the sense that there had been numerous calls from concerned members of the public to the radio station. Many village schools had been closed as a precautionary measure, and the police had warned people living in remote areas to remain vigilant if venturing out after nightfall.

After having briefly consulted his map in order to ascertain the whereabouts and easiest means of getting to Thelford, Montrose got in his vehicle and reversed out of his drive. He reckoned it would take him just under half an hour to get there, providing the roads were clear and he did not get stuck behind a tractor — as always seemed to be the case whenever he drove out along these narrow country roads.

Numerous rural villages passed by, many with their own pillar boxes set outside or near their village shops; and he could not help but think, with something of a wry grin, that people were now far more cautious whenever they approached them. He pulled into the village shop layby in one such place — Lower Steepleton — and got out of his vehicle. An elderly grey-haired woman was outside binning some rubbish.

'Good morning,' said Montrose.

'Oh, hello,' the woman greeted casually before going back inside.

Montrose followed her, a bell tinkling as he opened the door.

The shop was like many other little village shops he had been in: neat, orderly, and efficiently run. It clearly offered a much-needed service to the local inhabitants.

'Anything I can help you with?' asked the woman from behind the counter.

'Yes. Do you by chance have a tape measure?' Montrose asked.

'Why, yes, I think we do.' The shopkeeper went to some shelves at the rear of the shop and returned. 'I'm afraid it's not the metal retractable kind.'

'This will do just fine.' Montrose

counted out the money, paid her, took the tape measure and left the shop. Outside, he went up to the pillar box and, with a quick glance around to make sure no one was watching him, began measuring it.

It was sixty inches from top to base and had a circumference of forty-eight inches. Without access to the police reports and going purely on what he had heard on the news, he came to the rationalisation that the bodies had probably been dismembered in order to fit. He doubted whether even a pygmy contortionist could get inside whole.

A door opened nearby and an old man came shuffling out.

Montrose quickly pocketed his tape measure and nonchalantly headed back to his vehicle. He got in and continued his drive to Thelford.

Upon arrival in the village, he saw that there were police incident signs up on the approach to the main street. He parked in the grounds of the village hall and, after checking that he had some fake identification on his person, set off for the Swan public house he had passed on the way in.

Several grizzled, unfriendly-looking faces turned as he went inside and strode up to the bar. There was an atmosphere here that sent a ripple of unease through him, as though his every move was being carefully watched. He put it down to the fact that there had been a nasty murder committed here and it was only natural that people would be on edge.

In these small, close-knit communities, where everyone had known everyone else for decades, it stood to reason that the presence of a stranger the day after something like this was bound to raise hackles.

'All right?' greeted the hatchet-faced barman with a brusque nod.

'Good day to you. My name's Ray Smith. I work for The Oxford Investigator.'

The barman gave a disgruntled sigh. 'So you're another bloody reporter, are you? I thought as much as soon as I saw you come in.'

'I take it there's been quite a few then?' asked Montrose. He was relieved to see that many of the suspicious gazes were no longer directed at him.

'You could say that.' The barman ran a hand down his unshaven chin. 'So what'll it be?'

Montrose briefly examined the ales on tap. 'I'll have a pint of your best bitter and a packet of salt and vinegar crisps.' He had planned on having lunch here, but as there were no menus visible he was forced to conclude that they did not serve food.

Taking the payment, the barman handed the drink and the bag of crisps to his customer. 'If it's news you're after you'd be best talking to Wobbler. He'll be in shortly.'

'Wobbler?' Montrose cocked an eyebrow.

'It were him who found the poor bugger.'

'I see. I assume you've had the police crawling all over the place?'

'That we have. There were four police cars parked in the village hall last night and there were two there this morning.'

'I didn't see any.'

'Well, maybe they've gone for lunch,' replied the barman. 'And including you there's been at least a dozen reporters swarming around the place asking questions left, right and centre. And I'll tell you what I told them. Whoever murdered Jason Bennet had better get as far from Thelford as they can. He were in with a bad crowd, but they looked after their own from what someone told me. Mark my words, there'll be hell to pay before this is all over — and I'm talking literally.'

Montrose now had a name for the second victim. 'You said he was in with a bad crowd? Would you care to elaborate?' He took a sip from his drink.

The barman looked around furtively. He leaned closer. 'Devil worshippers,' he whispered.

Montrose almost spat out his beer. He did not know how to respond. He had expected the other to reveal that the victim had belonged to some drug-running gang or even the local shotgun club — but devil worshippers? That was a new one and no mistake.

'You heard me right. It was fairly common knowledge in the village.' The barman lowered his voice even further. There was a scared look in his eyes, but at the same time it seemed as though he wanted to tell his account no matter the cost.

'There used to be, and I assume still is, a place up in the nearby woods where on moonlit nights they'd all gather. At first folk thought it were just a bit of harmless fun, a bit daft maybe, but nothing to be that concerned with. Then things turned a bit sinister. Cats started disappearing. Dogs too. How long this went on for I couldn't say, but it reached its peak a few years ago when one night Ernie Shackleton's thirteen-year-old daughter went missing. The whole village mounted a search party. Police dogs and even the helicopter were brought in.

'They never found her, but they uncovered a clearing in the woods that had been used for black magic. There was an altar atop which were dead cats and all sorts, and — ' The barman paused upon seeing the main door open. 'Ah, here's Wobbler now . . . and his brother, Spud. I'll introduce you. Wobbler's basking somewhat in his newfound celebrity status.'

Wobbler was about as rustic an individual as Montrose had ever met. He was a short man, five foot three if that, and scruffier and more wizened than William 'Compo' Simmonite from the television show Last of the Summer Wine. He was dressed in a pair of torn tweed trousers; a coarse, grey-green jumper that looked as though it had been knitted from pig bristles; and a shapeless, sack-like felt hat. His boots were muddy and covered in dry cow dung. His dirty, bespectacled face was as round and as ruddy as a freshly dug beetroot, which, along with his shabby attire, made him look like a scarecrow that had clambered down from its post. He must have been about seventy. The even smaller, bearded man beside him looked older and as equally unkempt.

'What'll it be, Wobbler? The usual?' asked the barman.

Wobbler nodded.

'Here, let me get these,' said Montrose, reaching for his wallet.

'That's mighty decent of you, mister,' said Wobbler. There was a beery stench to

his breath and it was pretty obvious that he had been drinking prior to entering the public house.

Montrose took out several pound notes and bought a round of drinks for the two disreputable newcomers.

'This man's another reporter,' said the barman. 'I told him that it was you as found the body.' He handed the drinks over.

'That it were,' the rustic acknowledged proudly. He slurped nosily from his beer as did his sibling. Wiping away a moustache of froth, he placed his pint on the bar and began scratching at his ribs. 'Horrible, it were. Worst thing I've ever seen.'

Montrose stepped back a pace, certain that the man had fleas. 'Anything else you can tell me about it?'

'Oh, yes. There is at that.'

'Well, do you want to take a seat?' Montrose gestured to one of the empty tables.

'No, I'm better off standing. My piles have been playing havoc the last few days or so and sitting on one of these wooden

chairs is the last thing I want to do right now.' Wobbler stopped his scratching and straightened his weird hat. It was a truly odd-looking article of clothing, yet somehow it befitted the man upon whose head it rested.

'It were that bastard Norton who done it!' spat Wobbler's brother, Spud, with hard-to-contain rage. 'He's killed before. Now he's done it again. You know what they say — once a killer always a killer.' His words had to fight their way through his beard to be heard, and even then they were hard to make out due to his many missing teeth.

'I'd be careful making accusations like that, Spud,' cautioned the barman. 'Mr. Norton may not be that well-liked around Thelford but he's a powerful man, with many high-up friends.'

'Let him hear!' cried Spud, keen to promote his scurrilous agenda. 'It were him that did it!' There was a fire in his rheumy eyes, and he gripped his pint so tightly in his knobbly fist that Montrose thought it was going to shatter.

'Norton's got nothing to do with it!'

41

proclaimed Wobbler, adamantly disagreeing with his brother. 'He might be a bastard and he might've served his time for killing somebody back in the fifties, but it wasn't him who chopped up Bennet and put him in that postbox. For starters, he wouldn't dare. I bet even now he's scared stiff that those black magic folk think that he's the murderer; thinking that they're going to hunt him down and carve him up on that altar of theirs. After all, Bennet was one of their chosen ones, you know.'

Montrose had brought out his notebook and scribbled down some of the details. The thought that there might be an occult angle to these atrocities had got him interested, for he had initially not even considered the possibility that these could be ritual killings. From his reading on the subject he was only too well aware that this was an angle well worth considering. 'Who is this Mr. Norton?' he asked.

'Alaric Norton's a retired bank manager. He lives in the manor house,' the barman answered.

'Maybe I should pay him a visit,' said Montrose, thoughtfully pulling at his bottom lip.

'You'd be wasting your time,' said Wobbler. 'Like I said, he's got nothing to do with it.'

'Well, I guess he's innocent until proven guilty.' Montrose decided to change tack. Noticing that his informant was already close to finishing his drink, he ordered another round before turning to Wobbler once more. 'Regarding the body — can you tell me the circumstances behind the discovery? Tell me what you actually found.'

'What I found? What do you think I found?'

'I don't know. You tell me.' Montrose watched, mildly disgusted as Spud reached into a pocket and scratched at his nether regions. He half-expected the other to whisk out a ferret or something even more unsavoury, such as a mouldy, half-eaten, week-old cheese and pickle sandwich.

'Well it were like this, see. It were about half-past five, and I'd just parked my bike at the corner of the road outside the war memorial when I noticed that the door of the postbox was slightly ajar. Now normally there's a mail collection at four o'clock, but our postie's been off sick so I thought I'd better go and lock it. Didn't want any old Dick or Harry rummaging through other folks' letters. Anyhow, when I got closer I saw that there was something running down the outside.

'Now as you know, postboxes are red, but the base is black, and it was this that had been stained. I thought to myself, 'I hope that's paint,' but I knew that it wasn't. That was when I saw the foot. Christ! It didn't half give me a turn.'

Wobbler took a hearty glug from his pint.

'John Doyle, the landlord over at the Wheatsheaf in Little Warborough, was on the other side of the road. I shouted him over and together the two of us opened the postbox.' He paused for effect. 'And that was when Jason Bennet — or rather his arms and legs — fell out. His torso was still wedged inside. I'm not kidding you, it were like something from a horror film.'

'What did you do then?' asked Montrose.

'I can't say for sure. Guess I might've soiled my pants. And so would you if you'd seen what I saw. Doyle must've gone into the post office and called for the police.'

'Anything more you can tell me about the — ' Montrose stopped in mid-sentence upon seeing two uniformed police officers enter. 'Excuse me. I have to go to the toilet.' It was high time for him to make good his escape. Putting down his unfinished drink, he turned and slinked out the rear exit.

★　★　★

That evening Montrose sat upright in his bed, going through one of his murder books in a search for clues relating to the thought processes of the being he was tracking. From his study of the topic, he knew there was no single factor to explain why people carried out evil acts. People killed for money, power, revenge, passion, pleasure, or for other reasons that no one sane could possibly fathom.

Similarly, there was no single dominating trait which could be attributed to the many killers he had read about. Some were tragic loners — social outcasts and misfits who lived reclusive lives, whilst others were active members of society. Many hid behind guises — alternate personalities which enabled them to exist in worlds divorced from reality. In numerous cases one of the contributory factors had been dysfunctional childhood development brought about by the untimely death of one or both parents, abuse, or neglect.

Poring over his books, the relentless ticking from the clocks in his spare bedroom going through his ears like the sound of a thousand deathwatch beetles, it never for a moment dawned on him that he him himself fitted many of the criteria.

He began reading about Ed Gein, the infamous real-life Wisconsin ghoul who had murdered two women and dug up many more, fashioning macabre trinkets, household decorations, and even articles of attire out of their remains. A recluse with an unhealthy mother/son relationship, Gein's sickening crimes had gone on to inspire two of his favourite films — Alfred Hitchcock's Psycho and Tobe Hooper's The Texas Chainsaw Massacre. He had watched both over a dozen times and had never understood why the latter had been a banned movie. Each film had tried to portray the diametrically opposed aspects of Gein — from Norman Bates's disturbed normality to Leatherface's horrendous, inhuman monstrosity. Two portraits of insanity.

Did all that was transpiring in this case just boil down to insanity?

He did not think so. As motives went, that was pretty lame.

Then again, there was the Satanic link — although he did not give much credence to that. After all, there was nothing to suggest a connection with the first victim. Still, it was an avenue of investigation that he would not, as things currently stood, rule out. It seemed to him that Jason Bennet, like Pinky Whelps, had just been unfortunate in that he had

47

been in the wrong place at the wrong time. Victims of an opportunist — and as such, it was imperative that he made steps in finding out the motive which drove him.

Or her. Although he doubted that the murderer was female, it would be remiss of him not to consider that possibility. Some of the leading serial killers he had studied were women — notably Mary Ann Cotton, the most prolific serial killer in Victorian England, who was believed to have killed ten of her own children; and Belle Gunness, the Norwegian-born 'Black Widow' who had either poisoned her suitors or snuffed them out with a blow to the head from an axe. Yes, there was no denying the fact that the fairer sex could be just as dangerous.

Montrose cursed with frustration. Everything was too sketchy. He needed more to go on. He took some comfort from the likelihood that more bodies would be discovered.

He had consulted a detailed map of the area and had been somewhat dismayed at just how many little villages there were.

Well over a hundred. If he were to try and opt for a successful stakeout without anything else to go on, his chances of success would be more or less negligible. It would be like finding the proverbial needle in a haystack. It would be an utter waste of time; and what was more, he was only too well aware that the police were coordinating all their efforts to find the killer, just as he himself was, and he could only hope that he would beat them to it.

This was a race, and one in which there were no prizes for second place. On the few previous occasions when Montrose had solved murder cases before the police, he had sat back, smugly priding himself and feeling empowered by the knowledge that he alone knew the identity of the killer, and that for a while he held the other's fate in his hands. To surrender this information to the law and thus expose the murderer — and hence achieve popularity and perhaps even the goodwill of the nation — was not on his agenda. After all, he was no bounty hunter. Nor did it unduly trouble his conscience if the murderer struck again in the interim period between him figuring out who was responsible and the police making an arrest.

In some ways he likened himself to an angler — the sport was in the fishing and the catching and not so much in the eating of that which was caught. It was the unravelling, the unmasking, that — like his clockwork 'children' in the room next door — made him tick.

After having read something that would have brought nightmares to most normal people, Montrose put out his small bedside light and lay cold and alone in the dark, the curtain throwing eerie, dancing shadows across the room. His mind was cycling through countless dark possibilities and his eyes were focused on the small, open leaded window.

Out there somewhere, lurking in the gloom — perhaps even at the pillar box in his own village, the murderer could be in action. A blood-stained sack could be being offloaded from the boot of a vehicle by a shadowy figure. To Montrose, it was a pleasing thought.

3

The exploits of the Postbox Killer, as the murderer became known, were, not surprisingly, big news. Although so far he or she had only struck twice, the brutality and bizarre nature of the disposal of the victims had gripped the nation. Daily police briefings were shown on television amid lame reassurances to the public that all was being done to apprehend the killer.

In an effort to control the almost tangible sense of panic, Detective Chief Inspector Holbrooke made numerous spurious claims to the effect that it was really now only a matter of time before the law caught up with the individual concerned. In truth, he was floundering. There really was very little for him to go on.

The investigations into the lives of Pinky Whelps and Jason Bennet had turned up nothing. No one had a bad word to say about Whelps other than they were pretty sure he never disclosed his earnings to the Inland Revenue, and if everyone who did that ended up dead they would be awash with bodies by now. He had initially perked up when several people who knew Bennet had claimed that he was part of a weird group of devil worshippers, but after interviewing Bennet's friends he had quickly come to the conclusion that the meetings in the woods had more to do with smoking pot and getting away from the missus than anything occult.

The victim had worked as a book-keeper and had lived a rather dull life with a wife who was more concerned about the fact that he had never bothered to take out life insurance than the fact that he had been brutally murdered.

Holbrooke would have dearly loved to be able to attribute the crime to Irene Bennet, but she had been at a WI meeting during the relevant hours and in any case was clearly lacking the physical strength required to have carried out the job. No, she was shrewish and charmless, but unfortunately innocent.

There also seemed to be no connection between the two victims other than their gender and size.

Holbrooke could imagine a faceless figure watching people, eyeing them up to see if they could be made to fit inside a pillar box. Perhaps that was the only criterion the killer had. All leads for people who had a motive to kill Whelps and Bennet had dried up. He could only hope that sooner rather than later some new piece of information would come to light or that the murderer would make some error of judgement — some slip-up — which would lead to their capture.

In the meantime, many of those villagers who lived close to where the atrocities had been committed lived in constant fear, and neighbours who had lived amicably alongside one another for years now eyed one another with varying levels of suspicion. Still, life had to go on; and slowly, as each day went by without incident and the initial shock diminished, the fear and level of heightened vigilance decreased.

* * *

The sun had yet to rise on a misty May morning several weeks after the dual discoveries of Pinky Whelps and Jason Bennet when nineteen-year-old Police Constable Ian Walker, a relatively inexperienced new recruit to the force, failed to achieve national renown and a much-needed promotion by cycling past a figure whom he assumed to be the postman busily sorting out the mail from the pillar box on the outskirts of Goddard's Cross.

He would later report to his superior officers that it had all happened so quickly, that it was foggier than it really had been, and that he had been focused on avoiding the numerous potholes on the country road. Regardless of the facts, it was only as he had entered the village proper a couple of minutes later that a little nagging suspicion prompted him to make inquiries in the post office. Therein, much to his shock, he had encountered the genuine postman smoking a cigarette and collecting his morning paper.

Less than five minutes later, after

having instructed the postmaster to notify the police station, Walker pedalled back with all due haste to the pillar box.

All was still: deathly, eerily so in the morning mist. Apart from himself, there was no one about.

Far away, cows could be heard lowing.

Gulping back his fear, Walker slowly approached the wrought-iron, five-foot-high symbol of death which in his mind the pillar box had now become. He dismounted from his bike and rested it against a barbed wire fence, wondering who in their right mind would put a pillar box a mile or so from the nearest house. In all likelihood it only served one farm.

Eyes wary, he scanned his surroundings, the fingers of his right hand tightening around the haft of his truncheon. A cold, unpleasant sweat trickled down his spine, dampening his smart shirt. There was a dryness in his throat and, for a fleeting moment, he had the impression that there were eyes watching him from within the mist and surrounding hedgerows.

'Is anyone there?' he called out.

There was no answer.

Common sense was screaming at him to hold back. Upholding the law and carrying out his duties were not worth dying for. If his suspicions were correct and the figure he had seen earlier had been the Postbox Killer, then confronting him openly was perhaps not a wise tactic. From all Walker had been told, he was a bloodthirsty maniac.

Yet, tempering that thought was the glory of making the arrest of the year.

Mustering his courage and aware that backup should now be on its way, he withdrew his truncheon from his belt and strode forward, his nerves wound up like a coiled spring. However, any idea of capturing the culprit and getting his name in the papers was instantly shattered upon seeing the sight that lay before him.

Although the initial discovery filled Walker with such a level of revulsion that he rapidly emptied his stomach of his breakfast, he could tell that he must have interrupted the murderer in the act for which he had claimed such notoriety. The body was terribly mutilated, dismembered like those which had been found previously. However, in this case, half of it — one arm and the torso — were inside the pillar box whilst both legs, and the remaining arm lay outside. Where a heap of letters should be was now a pair of fleshy white, freckled buttocks.

Gagging, a rivulet of sick leaking from between the fingers of the hand clamped to his mouth, the rookie policeman felt his knees weaken. He sagged down so that he was now mere inches from the discarded arm, watching in numbed, nauseated horror as a slug crept slowly over the bloodied wrist.

In the distance he could hear the sounds of an approaching squad car.

★　★　★

By twelve noon the mist had burnt off and it was warm and sunny. The fields surrounding Goddard's Cross had been systematically searched by one of the largest ever mobilised police forces in the county. Sniffer dogs and even a police helicopter had been brought in, but aside from some tyre impressions which may or may not have been attributable to the killer nothing of great significance was found.

Detective Chief Inspector Holbrooke stood by his car, sipping coffee which he had poured from a thermos flask, watching as the crime scene was, at his insistence, investigated one last time.

Five minutes later, Orton came over shaking his head. From the look on his face it was clear no breakthroughs would be forthcoming, at least not there and then.

'Anything?' Holbrooke asked hopefully.

'Pretty much the same as before — an initial blow to the skull. The dismemberment looks exactly the same. As far as the placement of the parts in the postbox goes, clearly the killer was rattled by the sight of Constable Walker. I don't doubt that whoever did this intended to cram the whole body inside. Obviously we'll see if we can find anything when we do the post-mortem, but I wouldn't be too hopeful if I were you. I'll also get someone to go through the tyre prints, but they're not clear so I'm not that optimistic.'

Holbrooke scratched his head. This was now the third murder and he had made little progress in solving this case. There was no doubt in his mind that it was the actions of one person. The hammer blow to the back of the head — something which had not been disclosed to the public — strongly suggested that it was not a copycat killing.

* * *

As the remains of the latest victim were being loaded onto a waiting ambulance, nine miles away Montrose was stalking through the woods that lay at the far corner of a broad swath of agricultural land on the outskirts of Thelford.

He had spent much of the past few weeks visiting many of the neighbouring villages, mapping their pillar boxes as well as frequenting their public houses in order to glean any snippets of relevant information before coming to the decision that he would investigate the devil worshipping element connected with the death of Jason Bennet. He had absolutely no belief in anything supernatural, but it was undeniable that many killers had been convinced of various outlandish ideas.

A visit to the main library in Oxford had furnished him with some basic facts about Satanists and the black mass, which was supposedly a sacrilegious parody of the Catholic mass. From what he had gathered, most of the source material for such beliefs and practices was actually fictional, owing more to Dennis Wheatley than Lucifer.

It had rained a little during the night and the forest floor was wet underfoot, with water dripping off the trees. Montrose flinched as a large droplet fell down the back of his neck, then continued his search. His diligence was rewarded when, damp and bedraggled, he finally found his way to a clearing. In the centre was a large, roughly flat boulder, and he could see hardened wax deposits at either end where it looked like large candles might have been placed. Running his hands over the stone, he wondered if it could possibly have been used as a makeshift butcher's table for hacking off the victims' limbs.

There were certainly no obvious blood-stains, although he supposed that the rain might have washed them away. Exploring the area surrounding the boulder, he found a few dog ends from cigarettes that could well have been dropped by policemen. The area had undoubtedly been searched by the authorities, for he could see that the ground had been trampled by many feet. As there had been nothing about ritual killings in the papers, he thought it likely that the police had considered the Satanism element a red herring, but he felt he still needed to check it out himself. He took a few photographs from various angles and turned to leave.

Standing at the edge of the clearing was a man with a shotgun — and it was levelled at Montrose.

'What are you doing here? This is private property,' the man said, his voice controlled and strong.

'I do beg your pardon,' Montrose replied, thinking furiously. Could this be the killer? His instincts were telling him otherwise, but he could be wrong. He paused as he tried to work out which alias would be the best to use.

While he thought, the shotgun-wielding man said: 'Another bloody reporter I'll bet, trying to make money out of Jason's death. Well, are you?'

'Not exactly. I work for The Oxford Investigator. We specialise in highlighting those crimes the police fail to solve or are struggling with.' Seeing the stranger's face darken further, he added: 'We've sometimes managed to find the culprit where the authorities have failed.' To his relief this lie had the desired effect. The shotgun was lowered a little.

'So you're a kind of private eye?'

'You could say that. Here's my card,' Montrose said, trying not to shake as he handed over his 'Ray Smith' business card.

'Ray Smith, eh?' The man examined it for longer than Montrose would have liked, then he passed it back. 'All right, but you still shouldn't be up here without permission. I'm Douglas Bennet, Jason's brother.'

'Oh, I'm truly sorry. I didn't mean any

disrespect,' Montrose said, managing to hide his excitement. This could be a stroke of luck if he did not blow it. 'Has there been a lot of press interest?' he asked, knowing full well that the family had refused to speak with reporters.

'I've chased off at least seven from the farm and Irene has gone to stay with her brother to get away from them. What exactly is your angle then?'

'We aren't a newspaper as such; we publish the facts of unsolved crimes, not the rumours and gossip, so that our readers — some of whom are actually in the force or recently retired from it — can suggest possible avenues of inquiry.' Montrose was warming to his performance, making it up as he went along. 'Since I joined the company we've helped to throw new light on many cases, which has led to the apprehension of several criminals.'

Bennet looked steadily at Montrose, who displayed nothing but earnest sincerity. 'Sounds a bit fishy to me, but it's no secret that the police don't have a clue who killed Jason. At least they've the sense to realise that no one who knew him could have done it.' His voice wavered a little and his hard expression softened very slightly. 'There was stupid gossip about Mr. Norton up at the manor house having some kind of grudge against Jason but that's rubbish. They were friends. Some people tried to stir up resentment against Norton, people with their own grudges.'

'I'd heard that Mr. Norton had been known to the police a long time ago,' Montrose ventured. 'That he'd served time in prison for murder.'

'You've heard wrong,' Bennet said bluntly. 'No doubt you've been talking to the Fairbridge brothers.'

'Would that be Wobbler . . . and Spud?' Montrose guessed.

'That's them! Lying scoundrels, both of them. It's well known that they've borne a grudge against Norton ever since he had Spud sent to court for poaching on his land. As far as this devil worshipping nonsense, well that's just a load of horse dung. Yeah, things went on here but that all died out years ago.'

'And the girl ... the one who vanished?'

'I suppose you're talking about Becky Shackleton?'

'Yes, the barman at the Swan told me — '

'Becky got fed up with Thelford and now she works evenings as a barmaid at the Plough over in Thurley,' Bennet interrupted. 'So you've also been talking to the village's biggest fibber, Ron Harding. He's the barman at the Swan.'

Montrose was temporarily confused. If his new informant was telling the truth — and that in itself was open to question — then it appeared that he had been told nothing but a pack of lies. It dawned on him that there was little more he could do here. 'Well thank you for telling me this. I suppose I'd better be going.'

'If you find out anything get in touch.' It was neither a question nor a statement, but a demand.

'Certainly.' Montrose edged back, unwilling to turn his back on the man with the shotgun. During the course of this investigation he had found no one whom he could trust. For all he knew, this man — who claimed to be one of the victim's brothers — could be just waiting for a chance to club him down. Montrose was reasonably confident he would not shoot, as that was not the murderer's modus operandi, but he could knock him out. After that the butchering tools would come out and it would be a pillar box for a grave.

He pulled back further and then, when he was content that there was enough distance between them, he turned and hurried away.

★ ★ ★

It was on the six o'clock evening news that Montrose — along with the rest of the population of the UK — learned that the Postbox Killer had struck a third time. The victim this time was identified as thirty-six-year-old schoolteacher, Matthew King, a married father of two from Longstock — a village some six miles from Goddard's Cross, where his dismembered body had been found.

The details of the murder as given out on the news bulletin were sketchy, for the police did not want to openly admit that one of their team had missed the chance of apprehending the killer. Such information would be disastrous for public trust.

Nevertheless, the news thrilled Montrose, for it had given him a new lead to investigate now that he had consigned the devil-worshipping exploits associated with Jason Bennet to the status of a red herring. He could only hope that the inhabitants of Goddard's Cross were not as scheming or as fraudulent in what they might disclose as the inhabitants of Thelford.

Montrose rose from his chair and was about to go over and turn the television channel to a documentary about the Nazi death camps when there came a firm rap on his front door. He went to see who it was. Opening the door, he took a rather startled step back upon seeing a policeman.

'Good evening, sir.'

'Yes. Good evening, constable,' Montrose mumbled. For some inexplicable reason he suddenly felt uncomfortable, guilty almost.

He swallowed nervously. 'Is there anything I can do for you?'

'I'm just conducting some door-to-door inquiries. It's to do with these postbox murders that have been happening hereabouts. I daresay you're familiar with them?'

Montrose nodded. 'Yes. A most terrible business.' Over the policeman's shoulder, he could see a second policeman questioning his neighbours on the other side of the cul-de-sac. All it would take would be for one of these people to voice their disapproval of him, perhaps providing the police with details of what they considered to be his eccentricities, and the next thing he knew he would be taken down to the station for an interrogation. With a deep breath, he tried to dismiss this paranoid thought.

'Indeed,' agreed the police constable. 'Well, we're here this evening just asking if anyone has seen anything, no matter how insignificant it may have seemed at the time, that might prove of assistance in capturing this murderer.'

Montrose shook his head. 'Nothing

untoward, I'm afraid. It's all very quiet here. Obviously if I see anything I'll let you know.'

'Very good. Sorry for interrupting your evening. Good night.'

Montrose closed the door and took a deep breath. His pulse was racing as he leant against the back of the door, listening to the sound of the policeman going away. His heart thudded like a caged animal in his ribcage and he felt sick. It was only then he realised that he had been holding his breath. He let it out in one long exhalation and then went back to his living room.

Were they on to him? Did the police know that he knew they were on to him? It would be just their kind of tactic — to prolong his assumption that they thought him innocent in the hope that by doing so they would expose his involvement in the search for the killer. But he would be damned if he would play out the rope by which they could metaphorically hang him.

Refute everything. That was the solution. After all, they had nothing on him . . . had they?

What were his neighbours telling them even now? That he was an oddball who lived alone. That he drove out at strange hours and was rarely seen. That he never greeted them or interacted with them in any way.

And what if the net was tightening further? The police would have undoubtedly quizzed the village landlords and post office workers, asking if any strangers had been seen lurking around — individuals behaving oddly or asking too many unhealthy questions about all of this. Surely Montrose's actions were blameless, but they could be misconstrued.

These were deeply uncomfortable thoughts.

One comforting notion, however, was the realisation that if the police were now having to resort to calling at people's doors, then it stood to reason that they were nowhere closer to unravelling this case. That they possessed more information and hard evidence than he did was undeniable; yet for all that and the resources they commanded, it appeared he could still beat them to solving this.

He went over to his drinks cabinet and poured himself a large measure of brandy. Having now lost interest in the television programme he had been so keen on viewing, Montrose retired to his workshop and study.

He peered out from his window, spying on the police as they began winding things up. He waited in the darkness, watching as they got into their police car and drove away before switching on the light.

On one wall he had hung up a large magnified map of the surrounding area. Long Gallop and Thelford were ringed in red pen. A few scribbled notes were pinned nearby. He searched for a few seconds before finding Goddard's Cross. This too he circled in red.

Apart from the fact that all were within a twenty-mile geographical spread, there seemed to be no obvious pattern emerging — at least none concerning the spatial distribution of the location of the victims.

He stepped back from the map, wondering briefly how it would look covered in red rings if the murderer were to strike time and time again; if his or her killing spree were to go on unchecked. It was possible.

* * *

It had just gone eleven o'clock when Jim Morton and his drinking pal, known only as Oz, left the Dead Duck public house on the fringe of the Ryfield Estate, four miles from Thelford. They were the last to leave and all evening the gossip by the bar had concerned the Postbox Killer and the latest victim which had been discovered that morning.

'Makes you wonder who's going to be next, don't it?' slurred Oz. He had been drinking steadily since lunchtime, and for him the pavement was now more like the surface of a bouncy castle. His mind and vision were swimming

'The sooner that bugger's caught the better,' replied Morton.

'Say . . . look. There's the . . . post-box . . . ' Oz pointed to the object in question, which was bathed in the yellow light that shone from a nearby lamp-post. He hiccoughed and staggered back a step but his friend, who had years of practice in doing so, supported him. 'What do you think's inside?'

'Come on, Oz. Time for bed.' Morton tried to steer him away but to no avail. He was still relatively sober and he had no real compulsion to go looking for dead bodies. Not that he expected to find any, but it was best not to tempt fate too much.

'Let's just have a butcher's.'

'Can't we just go?'

'I just want to take a peek.'

'A leak more likely,' quipped Morton. 'You should have gone before we left.' If he had a pound for the number of times his friend had urinated in public he could have bought the Dead Duck and saved both of them the inconvenience of coming out of an evening.

'It's this cold night air.'

'So it's nothing to do with the twenty or so pints you've drunk today?

Oz hiccoughed again. 'I just want to take a look. There's no harm in that, surely?'

'Okay . . . and then I'll take you home.'

'That's fine. Now come on . . . I want to make sure that . . . ' Unsteadily, Oz broke free of his friend's hold and lurched across the road. He began unbuckling his belt and that was when he stumbled on the kerb and fell, arms outstretched, towards the pillar box, embracing it. Immediately, even in his intoxicated state, he reeled back.

A pair of blood-filled eyes stared out from the darkened letter opening.

4

It was a quarter past six in the morning when Orton whisked back the blue sheet to reveal the dismembered remains of the latest victim, who now lay spread out on the operating table in the police morgue. He had been identified as fifty-one-year-old taxi driver Peter Jenkins.

Holbrooke looked on, a grim set to his jaw.

'Like I told you on the phone, James, there's a difference,' said Orton. With his pen, he pointed to a series of bruised blue-black marks around the cadaver's neck. 'He's been strangled. There's no sign of a blow to the head. Unlike the others, there are also signs that he may have put up a bit of a struggle. Note the bruised bottom lip and the grazed knuckles on his right hand.'

'You think he might have landed a punch on his attacker?'

'Quite probably, for all the good it did him.'

'What about the removal of the limbs? Is that the same?' Holbrooke was dubious as to whether this slaying could be attributed to the same murderer. It was unusual, though not unprecedented, for the method of killing to become inconsistent.

'Yes.'

'So you don't think it was a copycat?'

'My conclusion is that, whereas before the killer succeeded in knocking out his — and I say his with some certainty — victim with one blow, I think this time he failed to take his target unawares. There was a scuffle. Maybe the hammer or lead piping was lost, resulting in the killer being forced to use his bare hands. There's also the coincidence of the date.'

Holbrooke looked confused.

'Both pairs of murders were committed at some time on the second of the month. It might just be coincidental but I doubt it.'

'You know we have to get this bastard soon.' There was a venomous tone to Holbrooke's voice. 'The chief superintendent's breathing down my neck, especially

76

after that fiasco with young Constable Walker. How on earth he wasn't even able to provide us with a decent photo-fit is beyond me. I mean, have you seen it? My five-year-old daughter could do better. Makes you wonder just what he did at Hendon.' With some level of annoyance, he realised that the forensic scientist appeared to be distracted, his eyes scrutinising the corpse anew. 'Are you listening to me?'

Orton sighed. 'Sorry, I just keep thinking that maybe I've missed something. Anyway, the time of death is very similar to the others: only a few hours before the discovery of the body, which in this case puts it at between noon and about six o'clock yesterday evening.'

'Which fits with what we know. Jenkins finished his shift at the taxi rank at two in the afternoon and never made it home. He always walked back to his house and the route took him along a couple of quiet roads. I'd guess that he was attacked there, carted into the back of a van or something, and that was the end of him.

'I've got my officers out searching the

whole route, and there'll be a piece on the evening news asking if anyone saw him on his walk. It's possible we could turn something up.' Holbrooke stepped back from the body parts and stood with his hands in his pockets, brooding. 'Four people dead and we're not even close to an arrest.'

'Don't you have any theories at all?' Orton asked.

'There are all manner of ideas flying round this bloody station. Just sit in the canteen and you'll hear them — from the return of Jack the Ripper to a vengeful ex-post office worker. Hell — Stanford, who works in the patrol department, reckons it might be a disgruntled centenarian whose telegram from the Queen never arrived in time for her birthday celebrations. To tell you the truth, I don't know where I'm going with this one.

'There's no evidence except the bodies themselves, and they don't tell us much. All you can give me is that the killer's likely to be a man! The individual murders really don't seem to be personal, so that's put a whole lot of suspects out of the equation — all the 'who benefits' stuff just doesn't apply here.'

'I take it you've looked at all the victims from that point of view?'

'Or course I have,' Holbrooke answered tetchily. 'Every possible culprit either has a really good alibi or had no reason to kill the victim at all. I was hopeful about that brother of Jason Bennet's for a while. He narrowly escaped a custodial sentence for GBH when he was a youngster. However, he was bidding on some farm equipment in Aylesbury all that day and a barn filled with farmers can testify to it.'

'There is one thing that might give you some hope,' Orton said.

'Well, I'm a long time off retirement, so it can't be that!'

Orton ignored the joke. 'Our killer is starting to make mistakes. He nearly got spotted by young Walker when he left Mr. King half out of the postbox. And this one — ' He pointed at Jenkins's corpse. ' — nearly got away from him. I'd say that all the luck was on his side to begin with, but it may be starting to change. If he stops now I wouldn't be surprised if we never get him; but if he has the compulsion to carry on killing, which I suspect he has, then his luck's going to run out sometime.'

'So what you're saying is that by the time we reach the twentieth or so corpse we should get him! Bloody hell, Stan!' Holbrooke exclaimed. 'I can't just sit and wait!'

'Go back to your investigations then, James, and I sincerely hope that you get him before the second of June. If not, I think I'll have another jigsaw job on my slab before this is all over.'

★   ★   ★

There was a stiffness in Montrose's body when he got up that morning and, swinging his legs out of bed, he felt an acute ache in his ribs. He had not slept well, and he had a vague memory of having gone downstairs during the night for a glass of milk. Perhaps he had inadvertently stumbled against the edge of a cupboard or something. Lifting his pyjama top, he winced at the ugly-looking bruise just below his left nipple. It looked and felt as though someone had given him a right hook.

He took some painkillers, then made himself some breakfast and settled down to watch the news.

His aches and pains were instantly forgotten upon hearing that a fourth body had been found unceremoniously dumped inside a pillar box.

There was a pattern developing, of that he was certain. Just as before — two murders on the same day. What was more, both had been found on the same date, exactly one month apart. The third day of April and the third day of May.

Montrose consulted his diary on the off chance there was anything special about the dates — full moon, special saint's days, public holidays. Nothing.

Of course he had no direct way of knowing, short of somehow gaining access to the official police medical reports, whether those dates matched the actual time of death. The news bulletins had given little away, so for all he knew the deposited bodies could have been several days old prior to their unusual interment. However, he suspected that was not the case. In all likelihood they had been killed on the second and deposited the day after.

For the rest of the morning, Montrose busied himself in his workshop. There were several more clocks that needed fixing and he was getting behind, such was his preoccupation with the ongoing murder case.

At half-past eleven he stopped what he was doing, went downstairs and prepared himself a quick lunch. He then settled down to watch the news. It was during the course of the bulletin that the name of the latest victim was revealed: Peter Jenkins.

Montrose stared at the screen, mouth agape; his sausage, pronged on his fork, halfway towards his mouth. He had known this man — a taxi driver from the notorious Ryfield Estate. Despite his rather mundane profession, Jenkins had also been an avid collector of antique carriage clocks. Montrose had done some work for him over the years. In fact, he thought he had one or two of Jenkins's clocks upstairs still waiting to be stripped down and taken apart, prior to reassembly.

Stripped down and taken apart.

Mentally, he likened one of his deconstructed clocks to how the unfortunate Jenkins must now look. The internal workings — the cogs, springs, sprockets, hands, levers, pendulums, dials and all — were red and splotchy. Bloody organs.

He tried to clear his mind. Such thoughts were most unhealthy.

Obscenely, a thick dollop of tomato ketchup blobbed from his sausage and fell onto his plate. He put his fork down, unable to finish his meal. Clearly the identification of the victim had some deep effect on him, for he sat there gazing absently at the remains of his lunch for a good five minutes before regaining some measure of lucidity.

What he needed was a plan of action.

Perhaps if he waited till after the police had completed their bit of snooping, he could go and do some investigating of his own.

That idea had just flashed through his mind when a second thought struck him, one that disturbed him profoundly.

It was highly probable that, having ascertained the identity of the latest victim, the police would follow the trail of Jenkins's contacts to wherever they might lead. One strand of his past acquaintances led to a certain clock repairer. Any police detective worth his salt would be able to trace that.

Montrose sprang from his seat and dashed to the lounge window. Aware that his hand was shaking, he peeled back a section of curtain and peered out, half-expecting to see shadowy figures edging around the rear of the house as others prepared to batter down the door and storm inside.

Fortunately for him there was no one there.

★   ★   ★

It was approaching three o'clock in the afternoon and Detective Chief Inspector Holbrooke was busily going through

84

some paperwork when there came a firm knock on the door to his office. 'Enter,' he said, looking up from his desk.

Inspector Jackson walked in. Behind him was a lanky, sandy-haired man of about thirty. He was scruffy, unkempt and unshaven, his clothes casual and unwashed. It would not be at all surprising to discover that the man had tattoos and a pierced belly button. There was a gaunt look to him, like that of a half-dead rock star.

'Sir, we may have an important development. This is Mr. Edgar Craven. He's got some important information regarding the Postbox Killer,' Jackson announced.

Holbrooke's eyes lit up. 'Really?' He gestured to a chair. 'Come in, Mr. Craven, and take a seat.'

Craven stood there for a moment as though he was now having second thoughts about coming here in the first place. With reluctant steps, he made for the empty chair and sat down. 'I've seen him. I've seen the killer.' There was fear in his voice.

Holbrooke's eyes flickered to his inspector.

'He nearly got me. I'm lucky I'm not lying chopped up in a postbox waiting for someone to find.' Craven was on edge, fidgeting all the time, his eyes roving around the office as though expecting something malign to spring out of a filing cabinet. 'The bastard tried to pull me into his van. It must have been him. I'm sure of it.'

'Let's start from the beginning, shall we?' said Holbrooke. 'Where exactly did this all take place . . . and when?'

'It was as I was coming along the farm track on the outskirts of Maples Green. I'd been out fishing on the canal, you see.'

'When was this?' Holbrooke asked.

'Yesterday evening, about seven.'

'Okay.' Holbrooke nodded. 'Go on.'

'As I said, I was coming along the track heading for home when suddenly I was aware of something behind me. I turned and saw a small white van creeping its way very slowly in my direction. At first I thought it was just one of the farm labourers heading for a pint or two after

86

having done their shift, but I couldn't understand why it was hanging back all the time.

'I started to walk faster. The van speeded up. It was as though whoever was driving it wanted to keep a good eye on me. After a few minutes I stopped to tie a shoelace, and I waved him on, signalling to him that I'd stand aside so that he could pass by.' Craven paused, his eyes falling on the coffee-making machine in the corner of the room. 'Can I have a drink? My throat's very dry.'

'Sure.' Holbrooke signalled to his inspector. 'Tyrone, get him a coffee, would you?'

Jackson dutifully went over and fetched Craven a drink. It came in a plastic cup and had the consistency, and some said the taste, of tar. Nevertheless, Craven took a gulp. He placed the cup on the desk.

'Slowly the van came closer. It then pulled level and the driver's window was wound down.' He stopped and took a second lengthy drink from the steaming cup.

Holbrooke figured that the man must have a throat made from asbestos. He sat up in his chair. 'And then?'

'There was this really weird-looking man. I mean, if you think I'm odd-looking, you should have seen this guy. It was pretty obvious he was wearing some sort of disguise which looked as though it had just been put on: a false moustache and a black curly wig. He might have been wearing make-up as well. You know, that powder women sometimes pat their faces with. All he was missing was the red lipstick.

'I did a double-take and nearly fell into the ditch at the side of the road. That was when he leaned right out of the window and asked me if I could give him directions to Oxford.'

'To Oxford?' Holbrooke repeated lamely. He was now beginning to think that there was something wrong with his informant. He did not appear or sound the full shilling, although for the time being he was prepared to hear him out and put his strange account down to a claimed encounter with the prime suspect.

'Yes. I told him he was going in the wrong direction and that he would be better off heading to Thelford and then going north until he reached the main road. He just nodded. He then asked if I'd be on for getting in and showing him the quickest route. I thought, not bloody likely. I've seen some freaks in my time, having been to Stonehenge and numerous music festivals, but this guy put them all in the shade. He said he'd give me a fiver for any inconvenience caused but I said I had to be getting back.'

'How did he respond to that?' asked Holbrooke. Despite considering himself to be a good judge of character, he was still unable to reach a decision as to whether to believe this man or not. If he were to judge solely on the other's appearance he would be forced to conclude that it was all a load of codswallop.

'He went nuts! He threw the door open and reached out for me as if to try and grab me and pull me in. It was then that I saw his face proper. His eyes were soulless, black almost. I pulled back further and fell in the ditch. Suddenly the madman was back in his seat. He slammed the van door shut and sped off, kicking up a huge cloud of dust. That was when I saw a second van coming along from behind. This time it was one of the farm workers. Normally I don't get on with them, but by Christ was I happy to see him.'

'What about his accent?'

'No different from mine. Local, without doubt.'

So it was not anyone particularly cultured or educated, thought Holbrooke judgementally to himself. 'Any reason why you didn't report this incident yesterday?'

'I considered it. However, at first I thought it was just some loony who was high on drink or drugs. Then after learning of the two murders this morning on the news and the public appeal for help in finding the murderer, I thought I'd better report it.'

'You've done the right thing. Now let's go over this.' Holbrooke reached for a pad of paper and picked up a pen. 'Tyrone, get me a detailed map of the area, will you, so that Mr. Craven can show us the exact location where this happened.'

Jackson unfolded a map he had taken from a drawer. Craven pointed to the location. 'I'd say it was about here.'

'Did you get the vehicle's registration?' Holbrooke asked hopefully.

'I tried, but it looked to have been deliberately smeared over with mud.'

'I see. What about the make of the vehicle?'

'I'm afraid I know next to nothing about vans, or cars for that matter. I don't drive and I'd have trouble distinguishing a Mini from a Rolls Royce.'

Holbrooke sighed with mild disappointment. 'Okay. What about the driver, the man who attacked you? You said he was in disguise. Do you think, with the help of our police artists, that you could come up with a reasonable likeness?'

'Maybe. But like I said his features were largely masked by make-up and a false Groucho Marx moustache. It was his eyes, however. They were filled with madness.'

* * *

Montrose had never had reason to visit the Ryfield Estate before, but he knew it had a bad reputation. Whether it was warranted or not he had no means of knowing, but it was certainly a place most of the surrounding country folk avoided like the plague if at all possible.

He found it strange, going almost suddenly from quaint, bucolic hamlets with their thatched-roofed cottages and neat village greens — not to mention their wealthy inhabitants — to the drab conurbation with its grey, charmless and largely uniform houses. The few faces he saw were indicative of the social and economic dichotomy as well: drawn, haggard, drink-addled, and dejected. This really was the land of no hope, he thought to himself.

It took him a good ten minutes of driving around the litter-strewn streets before he reached the Dead Duck, the estate's only public house. Pulling into the car park, he knew he was in the right place on seeing the crowd of teenagers thronged around the pillar box on the other side of the road. It appeared as though the otherwise mundane feature had now been elevated to a macabre place of interest — a ghoulish shrine around which the local reprobates hovered like flies around a corpse.

Montrose grimaced, knowing it would be unlikely that he would be able to take a closer look whilst they were there. He got out of his vehicle and made sure to lock up. Trying not to draw any undue attention to himself, he walked nonchalantly to the front door of the public house, his nerves tensing a little, not knowing what to expect.

He stopped outside, a yard or so from the main door. This was a very different kind of establishment from the Fox and Hounds at Long Gallop or the Swan at Thelford. It was more like a working man's club.

Feeling more than a little intimidated and decidedly overdressed, Montrose pushed open the door, noting with a start that Jenkins's face was staring out at him from a poster asking anyone with information about the taxi driver's last walk home to contact the police.

It was busy inside and he was hit by the dense fog of acrid cigarette smoke that filled the room. He weaved between groups of rowdy drinkers, making his way to the bar where he hastily ordered a half-pint of bitter, and then retired to a small round table in a corner. It was not going to be necessary to start a conversation about the killing, for it seemed that everyone was talking about it. All he had to do was sit back, look inconspicuous, sip at his drink, and listen.

'I'm just saying, he could have driven the killer somewhere and spotted something. That's why he got picked.' A large man with a pendulous beer belly and impressive sideburns was holding forth to a small group.

'But what about the others? Did they suss him out? I don't think so. It's all just down to bad luck,' commented a weasel-faced man with a flat cap.

'Yeah, if you're a skinny bloke in the wrong place at the wrong time it's chop-chop and into the postbox with you.' The moustachioed speaker was a giant of a man with broad shoulders.

One of the man's companions clearly thought so too. 'We know you're safe enough, Frank. Christ, the killer would have to mince you to make you fit!'

A short burst of laughter was hurriedly toned down at a warning cough from the barman.

'Sorry, Tom,' Frank apologised on behalf of the group.

'Okay. Just have a bit more respect for the dead, would you? I saw what was in that postbox out there and it's no laughing matter.'

Montrose cursed silently. The last thing he wanted was for the drinkers to stop talking. He need not have worried though, for as soon as the barman had gone to the other end of the bar the group shuffled a little closer to the window and carried on discussing the vicious murder. He continued to listen in.

'I spoke to Morton this afternoon and he said that Oz was staggering over for a Jimmy Riddle when he saw those eyes staring out.'

'Jesus! I bet he had damp trousers after that!'

'What I want to know is, how the hell did the killer draw up, unload a corpse, jemmy open the postbox, and shove it in without anyone noticing? You'd think some bugger would've seen him. Just doesn't make sense to me.'

'I reckon he must've had someone helping him, keeping watch while he did it.'

'Do you think he had someone helping him? Two people could do it quicker than one.'

Montrose pondered that. He had already considered the possibility that the murderer had an accomplice. It was not very likely, as most killers of this kind worked alone, but it was something he would not rule out. He tuned back in to the conversation just in time to hear the one he had identified as 'Frank' talking about the time frame for the deposition of the body.

'Mick says he posted some letters just after six o'clock and there was nothing wrong with the postbox then.'

'Yes, but would you actually notice? I mean, Morton said that the door was wedged shut, and it was just seeing the eyes looking out at Oz that gave it away.'

'According to Mick, he felt funny at posting the letters at all and sort of had a peek inside first. Surely he'd have noticed a pair of staring eyes! The body must've been put there later on.'

'So, sometime between six and closing time.' The speaker let out a rush of air and shook his head in disbelief. 'Hell's teeth! That bloke must have some guts, I tell you. Anyone could have seen him.'

'Hang on though, Sam. If he did it about quarter to eleven he might get a clear twenty minutes or so.' Frank warmed to his theory. 'Everyone who's going to the pub has already got there by then, and by that point none of us would be likely to leave until they were shutting up.'

Montrose felt a wave of excitement ripple through him. He had been struggling with this problem all day as it had seemed such an audacious act. Until this idea of Frank's, he had wondered whether the murderer was purposefully taking chances, perhaps actually wanting to be discovered, or whether the adrenaline of the danger was part of the attraction of such a public means of disposal.

If, however, the murderer had scouted out the Dead Duck on previous evenings and noticed this window of opportunity, then it was not so dangerous after all. It still took nerve of course, as there could have been kids out messing around late, but it was more of a calculated risk.

The conversation then veered off to a different subject; and after a few minutes of listening to a diatribe about the conditions at Frank's workplace, Montrose rose unobtrusively and wandered through to the only other room in the public house. Investing in a second half-pint, he found a discarded newspaper and a slightly sticky bench to sit on.

Opening out the paper, he pretended to read and let his ears start to pick out individual voices among the hubbub. Over the next twenty or so minutes, he heard that Jenkins had finished his shift as usual at six o'clock in the evening that day and had never made it home. A woman chatting to her friend was sure of this, as she had been enjoying the late sunshine in her garden and the now-dead taxi driver would have walked past her house as he always did. Apparently Jenkins was also a little deaf — a fact that Montrose had sometimes suspected in their own personal dealings. That could have made it easier for the murderer to attack him. From the details that had been released by the police, he knew they suspected that a very quiet stretch of road, a lane almost, was the place where Jenkins had been attacked.

Montrose suddenly felt he had heard enough. He quietly slipped out of the Dead Duck, glanced briefly at the infamous pillar box, and walked to where he had left his vehicle. It had been a fruitful evening and he had not needed to use his 'Ray Smith' business cards.

His mind turned towards the funeral of Jenkins, whenever it might be. It would be perfectly appropriate for him to attend it. After all he had known the deceased, however slightly, and if challenged could explain about the clocks that were still in his possession; although he would prefer not to mention these as he was rather hoping they might be overlooked by the deceased's next of kin. He was particularly taken by a small mid-Victorian carriage clock that would make a very good addition to his own collection.

Whistling softly to himself and wondering if his good black suit was still in the back of his wardrobe, he drove home.

5

A week had gone by since the discovery of the latest victims and there had still been no significant breakthroughs in apprehending the murderer.

Detective Chief Inspector Holbrooke came out of a long meeting to see Orton waiting by the door to his office.

'Well, how did it go?' enquired the forensic scientist.

'Not without a few hitches but otherwise okay. Seems that the high-ups have agreed to deploy more regional detectives to the case, so hopefully we won't be so thinly spread. They also agreed to assign more constables to patrol, and there's going to be increased numbers of unmarked cars doing the rounds as well. Even if we can't catch this bastard before he strikes again — on the second or third of next month if he sticks to his routine — then we have to make it nigh on impossible for him to get away with it.'

101

Holbrooke's eyes were drawn to the wanted poster which Craven had helped create and which was pinned to a notice board. It looked more like a caricature than a real person — a joke image; yet it was the best they had to go on at the present. There was also the name of the bogus investigator, 'Ray Smith', which had cropped up on several occasions in the course of the investigations. Subsequent checks had failed to associate him with any known investigatory body or newspaper, yet his presence had been noted at both Thelford and Long Gallop; and this fact alone interested those searching for the murderer.

'It'll be a tall order keeping an eye on every postbox in the county,' said Orton, stating the obvious. 'A very tall order. There must be several hundred of them.' He followed the other into his office.

'Don't you think I'm aware of that?' replied Holbrooke angrily. He paced over to the large map of the area, studying the pinpointed crime scenes — or rather the locations where victims had been found. What Orton said was true. There were well over a hundred villages scattered throughout the area, each with their own pillar box. To his surprise, there were also pillar boxes set in the middle of nowhere. In addition, after the discovery of Jenkins, it appeared that the murderer was no longer confining himself to purely rural areas. He was striking indiscriminately, almost at leisure, and that made him far more dangerous and unpredictable. 'Let's just hope that we have three weeks' respite before he kills again.' He went to his desk and sank down in his chair.

Orton poured himself a coffee. 'We could always see about closing down all the postboxes. Starve him of repositories for his body storage.'

'That was raised as a course of action but it's a non-starter. Not only would it have a profound effect on the postal service, it would also play right into the murderer's hands. It could be that that is exactly what he wants. At least that's how some of the others see it. Personally I think they're fools, but as I value my job I didn't argue with them. I'd say if this were to go on then things might change, but as it is they're not prepared to take such drastic measures.'

'Hmm. I figured that would be the case,' said Orton. 'So, as far as we're concerned, it's back to square one. We have to hope that some new piece of evidence comes to light in the interim.'

'I've assembled a team which I've appointed to chase up all the personal details of the four victims. It's just possible that there's a connection that we've somehow overlooked, some vital clue that links them all together. I think it's unlikely, and I'm still going on the supposition that they were all unfortunate victims of an opportunistic psychopath, more so after Craven's account. A pity he never got a good look at that registration plate. Still, we've narrowed down the field somewhat, and I've arranged for the traffic department to chase up all owners of white vans.'

'And don't forget we've got some tyre marks.' Orton took a sip from his plastic cup. 'It's not my field, but was anything mentioned about the psychology of the individual we're looking for?'

Holbrooke nodded. 'As far as trying to put together some kind of profile on the murderer, Winters reckons that we're looking for a psychopathic loner in his early- to mid-thirties. Someone relatively fit and probably involved in manual labour of some sort. A farmhand or a factory worker perhaps. Someone with an interest, or a fascination, or an obsession even, with taking things apart.

'As to why he's doing this, well that might be due to a desire for power which would be lacking from his mundane, day-to-day existence. Then again, it could well be a bid for recognition by an individual who feels unnoticed and unappreciated.'

'Why postboxes?'

'Winter seems to think that it could be down to the colour and its link with blood. He also thinks that there may be an intrinsic desire or need on the part of the murderer to 'contain' the victim. In some ways he likened it to a form of alternative burial, although I'm not sure I agree with him there. It was also suggested that the murderer may be putting the victims in postboxes as a means of mentally distancing himself from the actual crime.'

Orton's brow furrowed and he looked confused.

'Another of Winter's theories. He said that when someone posts something they do so in the knowledge that it is going to be sent elsewhere. And that once it's been posted — a letter or a parcel, for example — it's then out of the sender's hands. It becomes something which they can disassociate themselves from.' Holbrooke shrugged his shoulders. 'Personally I think it's just the actions of a complete and utter nutcase who is doing this purely for the shock value. We've not been able to find any other recorded instance of bodies in postboxes. It's a first.'

★ ★ ★

Fastidiously, Montrose peered through his fixed magnifying glass and, like some complex three-dimensional jigsaw puzzle, skilfully pieced the tiny components of the turn-of-the-century Waltham Traveller

106

pocketwatch back together. It took him well over an hour to do so, during which time he never once looked up or lost concentration, so absorbed was he in his work. His attention to every minute detail was uncanny.

Eventually, satisfied that it was now complete, he delicately closed the nickel case and brought it up to his eye, examining the outer surface for any scratches or signs of wear that would need touching up. He then raised it to his ear, listening attentively to the pulse of its mechanical heart; the steady, constant ticking. He felt a sense of elation born of the success of restoring life to that which had been dead, which for a moment made him feel like Mary Shelley's Victor Frankenstein. Returning the mended pocketwatch to the drawer from which he had taken it, he then left his workshop and went downstairs for a quick bite to eat.

He sat watching the news on his television whilst he ate his beans on toast. There were the now-daily updates regarding the Postbox Killer, but nothing new.

The police had released an image of the suspect but it was clear that the individual had been heavily disguised.

Still, they had narrowed it down to a white male probably in his mid-thirties and who spoke with a local accent. He was also using a white van as a means of transportation. The item had ended by warning members of the public to be especially vigilant when using rural lanes and byways and to be wary of strangers.

Once the news bulletin was over, Montrose switched the television off. He sat staring at the blank screen, wondering for a moment why the police had not informed the public of the fact that the murderer would not in all likelihood strike again until the second of next month. Was it so that they could root out and distinguish any copycat killing that might occur in the interim? It seemed unlikely but not altogether unprecedented. He knew that from his intensive study of the subject.

So the question was — what was he going to do now? There were still several lines of enquiry open to him, and he had already made some inroads in mapping out all of the pillar box locations in a ten-mile radius; details of which he had pinned to the map in his workshop

He knew from an obituary piece in the local newspaper that Jenkins's funeral was to be held at St. Mary's Church on the Ryfield Estate at three o'clock that very afternoon. That left him with a few hours to kill, which he did by going through some of his research books to see if he could learn anything that might be of relevance.

There was much to digest, but little of real significance apart from one glaring item which he cursed himself for overlooking and which set him all a jitter. That was the documented phenomenon of killers turning up at the funerals of those whom they had slain. There were several recorded incidents.

Could it be that the murderer would be someone amongst the mourners? It was a slim possibility which he had to cling to. Of course, the police could well be aware of this too and it was likely that they would be there . . . and, if so, could it not be that they would view him suspiciously? At least he had a valid reason to be there; but it would be prudent to remain inconspicuous as well as to keep an active level of vigilance for the killer.

At half-past two precisely he got in his vehicle and drove to the cemetery, where he parked in the layby outside. There were over three dozen funeral-goers there: men dressed in dark suits and women looking equally sombre in their attire. Old friends greeted one another with downcast gestures as a white-haired priest passed among them, sharing his condolences. People then began to drift into the church, from which solemn organ music was drifting out.

Montrose followed, his steps slow and measured, his head bowed slightly in a mock display of respect. He tried to remember the last time he had set foot inside a church, and his mind drew a blank until he belatedly realised it had only been a couple of months ago when he had attended his mother's funeral.

Finding himself at the rear of the shuffling procession, he looked around for a convenient place to see everyone else and, upon spotting an empty pew at the back of the church, he went to it and sat down.

The service lasted thirty minutes and Montrose became increasingly uneasy. He had never been religious, though from an early age his mother had tried her best to force her beliefs on him; and he found the whole procedure overtly sanctimonious, somewhat dull, and tedious.

Despite trying to keep his mind occupied by scanning those gathered, all he could see from where he sat was the backs of their heads. Two men got up and gave closing speeches, and then the coffin was being taken outside by the undertakers.

Montrose nipped out and skulked around the edge of the church to a place where he could surreptitiously watch those coming out. He was not sure exactly what it was he was looking for, but he believed he would know it when he saw it — maybe the uncontrollable twitch of a cheek muscle, or the nervous fidgeting of the hands, or even the guilty side-to-side flickering of the eyes. All tell-tale signs that things were not as innocent as they were being portrayed.

A cold chill ran down his spine as a sudden thought made him spin round. Was someone even now lurking else-where, spying on him? Was the watcher being watched? He gulped nervously. There were rows and rows of headstones, several statues, and a few tall marble memorials, but no sign of anyone.

At the edge of the cemetery, a hundred yards or so distant, there was a thick laurel hedge, and it was not inconceivable that someone could be concealed within, perhaps staring at him through a pair of binoculars. If so, what conclusion would they reach as to his actions? It was a disturbing thought.

If it was the police, then it would be only a matter of time before he found himself on the receiving end of some tough questions. And if it was the murderer . . .

Taking a firm mental grip on himself, Montrose decided that the best thing to do, given the circumstances, was to join the others while there was still time to do so without drawing undue attention to himself.

Nodding sadly to an elderly lady who gave him a half-hearted smile, he fell into rank as the mourners filed towards the burial plot. Once all had congregated, the priest gave a final eulogy and the coffin was lowered. Some sobbed and one woman wept openly as others fought to maintain a grip on their emotions.

And then it was over.

A few lingered, paying their last respects.

Montrose briefly contemplated whether he had the nerve, not to mention the bare-faced cheek, to go to the wake which, from the snippets of conversation he had heard, was going to be held at the Dead Duck — a decision that struck him as both fitting and a little macabre.

It was as he was giving this some thought, weighing up the various pros and cons of doing so, that he saw a man whom he had not noticed previously, either inside or exiting the church. He was dressed in a long black coat, which was unusual in itself, for it was neither cold or rainy; and he appeared to be scribbling down something in a pad.

The mysterious figure completed what he was doing and turned away.

★　★　★

In the darkness of his room, Montrose lay on his bed gazing up at the ceiling, his mind and body very much awake. Ever since leaving the cemetery that afternoon he had repeatedly gone over in his mind his course of action, ruminating over whether he had done the right thing or not.

At the time, he had been all up for pursuing the stranger and perhaps confronting him, demanding to know just what the other was up to; and yet in the end he had decided to get away, to make good his own escape on the suspicion that the enigmatic character could well have been a policeman carrying out a surveillance operation.

Now he was regretting his choice, whilst at the same time torturing his brain with the various ramifications.

What if the person he had seen was the murderer? Had the chance of identifying him slipped through his fingers? If he had held his nerve, could he now be the only person alive — aside from the killer himself — who could claim to know who the murderer was?

What if he had stalked the stranger? What would have been the outcome if things had turned ugly? And what had the man been jotting down in his book? Was that just a cover in case he was seen and questioned, enabling him to make out that he was a reporter?

Or maybe he had been drawing something; capturing a funereal tableau to keep for macabre prosperity. Stranger things had been recorded. Murderers, especially serial killers, were well known to keep 'trophies' of their victims — so why not a sketch of their victims being buried?

The ghoulish, grave-robbing exploits of the likes of Ed Gein aside, burial normally represented the final stage in the murder process. Was there some perverse fascination with a second burial; some facet of the killer's psyche which harboured some dark obsession with this? Was this linked with the duality aspect — two murders on the second of the month?

Like a tortured soul, Montrose knew that he would only find peace if he succeeded in solving the mystery of the Postbox Killer. His mind demanded answers, and he knew that when the time came — for he was certain there would be a next time — he would not lose his nerve as he had that afternoon. It would take an inordinate amount of courage and resolve — but if that was what was required, then so be it. He would get to the killer before the police did, or die trying.

* * *

Detective Chief Inspector Holbrooke was working late and he was feeling very weary. The relatives of all four victims had decided to join forces and had written a pointed letter explaining that, while they understood the difficulty of bringing the killer to justice, they did not believe that the police — and Holbrooke in particular — were doing all they could to make it happen.

Skimming through the letter for a second time, he felt sure that Douglas Bennet was the driving force behind it. The phrases were short and forceful, controlled but not at all placatory, just like the man himself.

Not that Holbrooke could blame them for getting angry; they had all lost loved ones — even Pinky Whelps had turned out to have had an aunt — and they had a point, for he was nowhere near an arrest. He and several other recently drafted-in detectives had trawled through the information about known criminals in the area and beyond who had concealed bodies, but there was no one that fitted the frame, and the only two men he could draw a comparison with were still in prison.

The best leads they had were a dodgy photo-fit and a generic white van to look out for. The traffic section would be able to get a list of owners for him, but it would be a long one; and it was very likely that the killer would either disguise or get rid of the van, now that it had been mentioned publicly.

The uniformed police would have a long job of it, checking out all local owners, and it might turn nothing up. Before the news about the van had been released he had sent out officers to the scrap merchants in the area to tell the owners to be on the lookout for anyone trying to offload a van of any description, but he did not hold out much hope there.

Holbrooke picked up the report from Constable Walker. He had sent the young policeman to watch the funeral of Jenkins on the off chance that the killer might turn up to it. Winters had raised this as a possibility and it was at least a positive thing they could do.

The rookie policeman had lurked nearby in an unmarked car and watched the mourners as they entered and left the church, but he had not been able to identify anyone. Apparently there were several men who could have been the one he saw on the morning of the third of May, but no one who stood out enough to merit further investigation.

Orton had been of no further help either. The killer had left nothing that could identify him on either the bodies or the pillar boxes and must have used gloves at all times. All four men had died several hours before their discovery, and Holbrooke had no doubt that each had been killed on the second day of the month.

That meant that the killer had managed to snatch and murder two people on the same day. He wondered what order it was done in — whether the killer drove around until he had two unconscious or dead victims in the van and then headed back elsewhere in order to cut them up, or if he did them one at a time.

Perhaps the killer actually chopped up the bodies in his van, thus avoiding any chance of incriminating evidence being found at his home — assuming they ever caught up with him, that was. The vehicle would probably be stored somewhere separate from the killer's home in that case to minimise the risk.

Surely when he went out to dispose of the bodies he would have both in the van together, along with a jemmy and a bolt-cutter, the latter used to cut out the wire cage from the pillar box.

Holbrooke had contacted the Royal Mail and arranged for an empty pillar box to be delivered to the station. He and a couple of his officers had borrowed a jemmy and bolt-cutters to see what was involved in breaking into it. The door was pretty easy to force open, and Constable Forton had clipped through the wires in a few seconds. They had used a shop mannequin with the limbs removed to replicate the next part and the whole job was completed in less than two minutes. They had stood there, grim-faced, unnerved by how easy it had been.

There was little more he could do until more evidence came to light. His comfortable home and blessedly normal family were only half an hour away, and Holbrooke needed a break from his office and the images this case conjured up.

Putting his papers away, he felt a pang

of guilt that he was able to leave the mystery alone for a while when four men had needed to be sewn back together again before they could be buried.

6

The murderous spree of the Postbox Killer was the last thing on thirty-nine-year-old Tom Hedley's mind as his car crested the hill on the outskirts of Todheath, a small village nestled in the Chilterns. He was travelling back from London, where he worked in the diplomatic service, and had spent the past few weeks in the Middle East doing things that were best not mentioned in public.

It had just gone two o'clock in the morning and he was keen to get home. There was no traffic on the road at this ungodly hour and that suited him fine.

Shifting gear, he allowed the car to accelerate on the downhill stretch as he approached the village, the bright head-lights picking out the darting shapes of rabbits and the occasional squashed hedgehog. It was then that he saw the parked car in the layby. A rotund, balding, bespectacled man with a shabby black suit and an out-of-place tie was trudging to a pillar box nearby, struggling under the weight of a large sack slung over his shoulders. The individual looked up, shock and surprise clearly imprinted all over his chubby face.

Hedley braked suddenly, although he would later testify that he did not know why he did so. After all, it was probably just the postman collecting mail — but something just did not seem right.

It was only as he got closer that he saw that the jacket the man was wearing was covered in bloodstains, as was the sack he carried. The man stood there, transfixed in the car headlights, his eyes uncannily wide behind the lenses of his glasses.

Hedley was just as frightened. Encounters like this did not happen during the normal course of things, especially not in this idyllic part of the Chilterns; not even in the slum areas of downtown Beirut and Baghdad — at least not that he was aware of. He had two courses of action.

He could either do the sensible thing and step on the accelerator and get the hell out of there and find a telephone box a safe distance away in order to inform the police . . . or he could play the hero and tackle the stranger. Some inner resolve made him go for the latter option. Unclipping his seatbelt, he threw the car door wide and leapt out.

The man with the sack cursed volubly and dropped his load.

'What the hell are you up to?' asked Hedley. He now stood less than five yards away from the other, close enough to see that the man was trembling.

Mouthing something meaningless, the fat man pulled back. With a series of cumbersome steps, he reached his parked car and fumbled with the driver's door.

It did not take a genius to tell that whatever was in the sack was definitely not mail. Hedley's stomach churned at the sight of the bulging, bloodied bag. Reasonably confident in his ability to tackle the other, he sprinted forward and, arms outstretched, caught the overweight man in a rugby tackle, hauling him to the damp ground.

The man may have been fat but he was

also strong. He shrugged off his attacker and scrambled to his feet. With a fleshy hand, he drew a long-bladed knife from a sheath at his belt.

Hedley crawled back on his arms and legs, righting himself several steps away.

The fat man hesitated. It was apparent that he was deliberating on either permanently silencing this witness to his crime or making a getaway. It seemed he had no real desire to fight. He edged back to his car, his flabby backside making contact with the bonnet, his knife held out before him in a warning to the other to keep his distance.

There was no doubt in Hedley's mind that he was now face to face with the murderer who had gained the dubious epithet of the Postbox Killer. To think that this porcine-faced, middle-aged nutcase was the cause of so much of the nation's fear would have been laughable under different circumstances, but here and now it was anything but.

'Say anything to the police about me and you're a dead man. Understand?' Keeping his eyes on Hedley, the killer made to get in his car a second time.

At his feet, obviously dropped by the fat man when he had been initially startled, Hedley saw a crowbar, no doubt the tool required for jemmying open the pillar box. In a fluid motion he dropped down, picked it up and threw it with all his might. It spun end over end before striking its target full in the face.

The killer yelled in agony and dropped his knife. Blood trickled from between the fingers clamped to his gashed forehead.

Hedley lunged forward. Catching the other by a raised trouser leg, he pulled hard. Fabric ripped as he dislodged the man from his car seat.

Screaming, the fat man landed painfully on his backside, his yellow underpants plain for all to see

Hedley waded in with a powerful kick, knowing full well that no court in the land would prosecute him for such violence when directed against this individual. He reached down and pulled the man half-upright by his scruffy tie before smacking him hard in the face with a clenched fist. He rained down another blow, breaking the murderer's glasses.

'Don't hurt me,' the man pleaded, raising his arms pathetically. 'Please don't hurt me!'

'You sick son of a bitch!' Hedley raised a fist threateningly, readying himself to drive in another punch. 'You're that bastard who's killed all those people over in Oxfordshire, aren't you? I ought to kill you right here and now and just say it was all in self-defence.'

'No . . . I . . . '

Hedley was about to launch a further attack when he saw headlights rounding a near curve in the road. Knowing that there was no more fight left in the other, he threw him forcibly to the ground and stepped out into the road in order to flag down the approaching motorist.

★　★　★

Detective Chief Inspector Holbrooke was in the process of drying himself down, having just stepped out of the shower, when he heard his wife calling him from downstairs. Hastily, he flung on his dressing gown and dashed out of the bathroom onto the landing.

'What is it?' he asked irritably, looking over the banister.

Anne Holbrooke looked up from the hallway, the telephone in her hand. 'It's Inspector Jackson. He sounds quite agitated.'

Holbrooke rushed down the stairs and took the telephone. 'Tyrone. How many times have — '

'We've got him, sir!' Jackson interrupted ecstatically. 'The Postbox Killer! He was arrested in the early hours of the morning over in Todheath, a village in the Chilterns. He's now being held over at the Aylesbury nick.'

'Are you . . . are you sure?' If this proved to be true then this would be the best piece of news Holbrooke had received that year.

'Without doubt. I've just been speaking to DCI Chambers at Aylesbury, and from what he told me the individual — who they've identified as fifty-seven-year-old Oliver Craddock — was caught red-handed, literally, by a member of the public.'

'Are you saying he was caught in the act? That he was disposing of a body at the time he was apprehended?'

'Exactly that. The details are still a bit sketchy, and as you're the lead investigator on this case DCI Chambers would rather converse with you before anything is made public. However, it seems that the culprit had a victim all ready to put in the postbox.'

'Anything on this Oliver Craddock?'

'I've no details as yet, apart from his age.'

'What about the victim?' With some measure of annoyance, Holbrooke noticed that his wife was listening in to his conversation, one of the reasons he disliked being called at home. He had always tried to keep his work and personal life separate. Still, given the reason for the telephone call, he had a lot to be pleased about.

'Again, no details.'

'Right.' Holbrooke had not had time to put on his wristwatch, so he glanced at the wall clock in the kitchen, seeing that it was approaching seven o'clock. 'I'll be in the office in an hour's time.'

'DCI Chambers has asked if you can get yourself over to the Aylesbury station. He's requested that Orton go as well.'

'Okay. I'll give Orton a call. Inform Chambers that we should be over there by half-eight, nine at the latest, depending on the traffic.' Holbrooke put the telephone down and, taking the stairs two at a time, hurried to his bedroom to get dressed.

★　★　★

The interview room was austere, dimly lit, and filled with a haze of grey-brown cigarette smoke which hovered around the ceiling.

Holbrooke had been briefed by Detective Chief Inspector Chambers prior to entering and he now sat as the other smoked, waiting for the suspect to be brought forth. There were several details about this enquiry which did not sit comfortably with him — not least that the victim had been a woman; Craddock's ex-wife, in fact. Orton had only just arrived and was now examining the body in the police morgue downstairs.

'He's admitted killing his wife but, as can be expected, he's adamantly protesting his innocence regarding the murders over in your patch.' Chambers stubbed out his cigarette and immediately lit another. Taking a deep drag, he then blew out a cloud of smoke from his nostrils. An old-school copper if ever there was one, he was no doubt relishing the prospect of claiming all the fame for having apprehended the Postbox Killer; and whereas Holbrooke was clean-shaven and smartly dressed, he was scruffy and sordid. There was also a hardness to his face indicative of someone who was not averse to using a bit of good old-fashioned police brutality in order to get the results he wanted.

'Maybe he's telling the truth,' suggested Holbrooke. 'After all, all the other victims have been men.'

'Telling the truth, my arse! He's got 'guilty' stamped all over his — ' Chambers stopped as a door was opened and Craddock was ushered inside by a police constable.

The defendant, his face battered,

limped forward and had just taken his seat when a sour-faced man carrying a black folder and a plastic cup of coffee entered the room and, upon noticing that there were no more seats, stood next to him. It was fairly clear that he was Craddock's lawyer.

Chambers switched on the tape recorder. 'Interview taking place on the twenty-third of May at nine twenty-seven. Present are DCI Holbrooke and DCI Chambers. Also present is the suspect's lawyer, Mark Hedges. State your name, age, address, and profession,' he ordered curtly.

Craddock looked at the lawyer, who gave him a nod. 'Oliver Mark Craddock. Fifty-seven. Ten Beckinsdale Avenue, Great Wootton. Financial adviser.' His words were rattled out and spoken rather mechanically, without variation in tone, inflection, or pitch.

'Good. Now then, you were seen by a member of the public in Todheath at or around half-past two this morning carrying a sack in which were found the dismembered remains of your ex-wife, Gabrielle Craddock. Your intention no doubt was to place her butchered body into the postbox, as you've done on four other occasions.' Chambers sucked smoke into his lungs. 'Now stop trying to squirm out of it and tell us the bloody truth. We all know that you're the Postbox Killer, so stop trying to deny it.'

'I had nothing to do with any of those other murders. I freely confess to — ' Craddock stopped immediately when his lawyer grabbed his shoulder.

'Any kind of man who would chop up his ex-missus is more than capable of having done this on more than one occasion. I know you did it. What I want to know is why you did it. So tell me!' Chambers grinned menacingly.

'I've told you all I'm going to say,' said Craddock.

Holbrooke could see the sweat standing out on the man's heavy-jowled face.

'You'll tell me everything I want to hear!' snarled Chambers. 'We've already established that your ex-wife had discovered that you were fiddling with the books. Making a nice little earner for yourself, were you? No doubt you found out and decided to top her. I guess it's only a matter of time before we find out that those other poor buggers had some dirt on you as well. Do yourself a favour and admit that you're the Postbox Killer.'

Craddock shifted uncomfortably in his chair as though it were now some kind of medieval torture device. 'I'm not the Postbox Killer! You know that as well as I do! You're just trying to pin this all on me. Okay, I'm going to jail, that's fair enough — but I'm not doing time for something I didn't do.'

'Mr. Craddock, remember what we — '

With a wave of a fleshy hand, Craddock brushed his lawyer's intervention aside. He knew that what he had done was indefensible, and he had already resigned himself to a very long stretch in prison.

'Yeah, so what if I killed her? The bitch deserved it. She was going around telling everyone just how inadequate I'd been as a husband. On top of all that she also found out that I was cooking the books. At first she was all set for making it known, and then she decided to start blackmailing me. I could only take so much.

'I snapped and pushed her down the stairs. Did I mean to kill her? I don't know, maybe I did. Anyhow, when I found her lying there, her neck broken, I knew I had to do something. I could have tried to make it look like an accident, but there was so much bad blood between us that I knew no one would believe that.

'So I came up with the idea of making her death look like one which could be attributed to the Postbox Killer in the hope that I'd get away with it.' His confession done, he hung his head low.

Chambers shook his head dismissively and turned questioningly to Holbrooke. 'What do you reckon?'

'Personally, I think he's telling the truth. And what's more . . . the real killer is still very much at large,' Holbrooke answered gravely. 'Although having said that, I think I'm going to reserve judgement until I hear from my forensic scientist. So if you'll excuse me . . . ' He got up and left the room.

'He did it, I'm sure of it!' Chambers called out, rising from his chair. He followed Holbrooke out into the corridor.

Holbrooke shook his head in disagreement. He was about to say something when he saw Orton coming towards them. 'Well?' he said.

'That didn't take long. There are so many differences from the killer's modus operandi that I can't, with any sense of credibility, assign any of this to the Postbox Killer. For one, the victim is a female — a notable departure. Secondly, the neck is broken, as are several bones in the left hand, which is indicative of a fall. Thirdly, the limbs have been sawn off, not hacked. Whoever did this was clearly trying to imitate the Postbox Killer. It's as blatant a copycat killing as I've ever seen.'

* * *

The small church at Longstock was almost overflowing with mourners attending the funeral of Matthew King. He had been a popular schoolteacher and the area in front of the altar was covered with floral tributes from his school as well as those of family and friends.

From his vantage point in a raised

gallery at the back of the church, overlooking the nave, Montrose watched, unprepared for the raw emotions he could see among the mourners. He had struggled with the decision to go to the funeral for days. On the one hand, he was worried that his presence at both this and Jenkins's send-off would be noted by the police. On the other, he had a theory he wanted to test out. He could not get the mysterious long-coated man out of his mind. In the few days that had followed the burial of Jenkins, Montrose had brooded over the possibility that he had seen the murderer and had failed to act. The frustration had built up until the pressure of it was too great — he had to go to King's funeral.

It had been lucky that King's funeral had taken longer to organise than Jenkins's, as Montrose had needed the time to work on a disguise for himself. His normal image was fairly smart but not too formal — dark trousers, a shirt, and a corduroy jacket most days. For the previous funeral he had worn his good black suit and, he felt, blended in well with the other mourners. He had also been able to say he had a right to be there. This time was different. He had no connection with the deceased — no valid one anyway, and he had gone to some trouble to look unlike himself.

A visit to a pawnbroker's shop in Oxford had furnished him with a slightly threadbare pair of black trousers and a dark jacket that had seen better days and was rather too big for him. He had even wondered briefly about dying his sandy hair dark or wearing a hat, but decided that both would look too noticeable, so he chose to stop shaving instead. His hair had always grown fast and after just five days he had enough stubble to make a passable beard. It was the best he could do to alter his appearance while still seeming normal, and it gave him a small amount of reassurance.

After the coffin was carried into the church the service started and, to Montrose's satisfaction, no one else had thought to sit upstairs. From his vantage point he scanned the crowd below, paying scant attention to the funeral itself other than to stand, sit, and kneel when everyone else did. He had placed himself in a corner to be out of the priest's line of sight, but this unfortunately had left a section of the church hidden from him.

His eyes going up and down the pews, he identified the immediate family very easily, and King's close friends seemed to be in the first few rows. He could not spot anyone who looked like the mysterious figure from Jenkins's funeral, but it was entirely possible that he was downstairs at the back of the church.

The more he thought about this, the more agitated he became. The gallery, which had seemed such a good choice at first, was useless if it shielded his quarry from him. There was also a very real chance that a few mourners would slip away in the minutes between the service and the burial.

Finally, moving as cautiously as he could, he edged away from his seat and stole silently down the stairs. These ended right at the back of the church and slightly to one side. Leaning back against the wall, he could see the last pews that had been hidden to him.

His heart lurched and began to race as he spotted a familiar figure sitting a few feet away. It was definitely the same man he had seen at Jenkins's funeral, the one who had been making notes or sketches. There had to be a connection. He was convinced it had to be either an undercover policeman or the killer himself.

The congregation suddenly rose as a final hymn began. At any moment the coffin would be carried out to the graveyard and Montrose would be stuck, waiting for the pallbearers to leave.

He quickly sidled out of the door, intending to find a good place outside to watch the proceedings. To his dismay, there was a young man positioned by the lych gate, his eyes fixed on the entrance to the church.

Montrose hastily pulled out a handkerchief and dabbed at his eyes, hoping the watcher would assume he had been overcome with grief. The young man might as well have been wearing his constable's uniform, it was so obvious that he was a policeman. He stood out like a sore thumb.

Torn between the urge to flee and his desire to follow his number-one suspect, Montrose dithered. As he waited uncertainly, the mourners appeared, following the coffin out of the church. He hung back, trying to look respectful while keeping watch for his suspect, and was relieved that no one gave him a second glance.

As the last stragglers exited the church, he received another shock. A tall, well-built man was among them. A man he had last seen in the woods around Thelford carrying a shotgun. Pulling back further into the shadows, he watched Douglas Bennet join the other mourners in their short walk to the grave of Matthew King.

What the hell was he doing here? Montrose felt himself start to panic. Fear was bubbling up inside him, threatening to take over. Had he totally misjudged Bennet? Could he actually be the anonymous killer, covering up fratricide by creating a series of murders? It was fantastical, bizarre — but could it be true? It would be an ingenious way of doing things if it were: to mask one crucial murder in a cauldron of others.

Just as Montrose was about to turn and run, to get away from the whole lot of them, he caught sight of someone else he recognised. He squinted a little, trying to be sure. Yes, it was the sister of Peter Jenkins, and she was now turning to speak with Bennet. So that was the connection.

He almost laughed with relief as the pieces fell into place. The families of the victims must have made contact with each other, either for solidarity or to put pressure on the police. There was nothing mysterious about their appearance at King's funeral. His heart slowed down to a more normal rate as the horrifying possibility that his instincts had been wrong about the Postbox Killer dissipated.

He felt so much better, in fact, that he almost missed the moment when his prime suspect strolled out of the church by a side door he had not noticed before.

Montrose straightened immediately and glanced towards the plainclothes policeman. The policeman was clearly a bit wet behind the ears and was currently looking in the other direction, so Montrose swiftly moved to follow his suspect. He only had a few seconds before the man would be out of sight, and sped up to make his way round the graveyard to a second gate that led out onto the street. The village of Longstock was quite large, and the main street had no less than three public houses as well as a grocer's and a butcher's.

The suspect let himself out, with Montrose following at a safe distance. He then headed past the Fleur de Lys and turned down a side road which Montrose knew led to a car park. His own vehicle was parked nearer to the church and he took the risky decision to dash back to it.

He drove it hurriedly to the Fleur de Lys and pulled in, hoping that the suspect had not yet made it to his own car and got well away.

A few tense minutes passed, but then he saw a brown saloon car pull out from the side road and he was able to see the driver clearly enough to know it was the man he wanted to follow. Gripping the steering wheel tightly, his knuckles whitening, Montrose pursued the brown car, trying to let a decent gap remain between them.

They drove out of Longstock and headed west. Several times a car got in front of Montrose and he welcomed it as a way to keep a low profile, but his hands were getting sweaty on the wheel and his head was starting to ache with the intense concentration of making sure the brown car did not get away from him. To his annoyance, they were reaching the market town of Farthingswell and traffic was building.

The tortuous one-way system that had recently been introduced was widely disliked and tended to cause tempers to flare. He had seen more than one low-speed collision where drivers had got confused. Sure enough, the town was busy. The brown car was separated from him by two others, and he was struggling to keep sight of it and still attend to driving safely.

A bus slipped in front of him with barely room to spare and he angrily leant on the horn. The driver raised a hand in a brief, insincere apology, leaving Montrose fuming. He flicked his eyes back to the line of traffic, looking for the brown car, but it was nowhere to be seen.

Sweat started to prickle his skin. Try as he might he could not see the car anywhere. The moment of inattention over the bus had cost him the pursuit. He swore volubly and battered a fist down on the steering wheel.

The line of traffic took him inexorably round the one-way system and he looked wildly in every direction, searching for his quarry, but to no avail. In a few minutes he had done the complete loop and was back where he had entered the town. He had to face it — he had lost the man he suspected to be the Postbox Killer and, in his excitement, he had even failed to catch the registration number. Not that it would have helped him much, as he had no means of accessing the police vehicle data bank.

There was nothing for it but to drive

home. His frustration spilled out into his driving and he was lucky not to have been spotted by the police, so erratic was his journey.

Finally arriving back at his cul-de-sac, he slammed the vehicle door and stormed into the house, never once noticing the brown car that had nosed smoothly into the road a short distance behind him.

7

May was disappearing and June approaching as late spring melded seamlessly and pleasantly into early summer. The weather forecasters all predicted it was going to be another hot one, although the record temperatures, droughts, and heatwaves of two years before were considered most unlikely. Many in the Home Counties were looking forward to the Henley Royal Regatta in just over a month's time, followed by Wimbledon a few weeks after that.

However, any ideas of a pin-striped blazer and a straw boater, never mind strawberries and cream, were far from Detective Chief Inspector Holbrooke's mind as he entered the large garage and surveyed the rusting, fire-blackened, battered wreck of a van. It looked exactly as he imagined it would when he had been informed of its retrieval a few hours ago. He saw Orton talking to a mechanic in oil-stained blue overalls and walked over to where they were.

The forensic scientist saw him approaching. 'It's in quite a state, isn't it? However, I've been able to establish a positive link with the tyre impressions found at Goddard's Cross.'

Holbrooke nodded and did a perambulation around the burnt-out vehicle, appraising the damage with his own eyes. He did a full circuit. 'Where exactly was it found?'

'In a patch of dense woodland close to Hatchwood Copse, three miles or so from Long Gallop where the first victim was found. There's a largely overgrown farm track which I doubt anyone uses anymore.

'As you can see, attempts have been made to set it on fire, to gut it completely. The registration plates have been removed and the vehicle identification number has been rasped off. The killer probably abandoned it shortly after that incident where Craven got away from him. But it's what's inside that's of interest.'

'Oh?' Holbrooke followed Orton round to the back of the van. 'Not another body, is it?'

'No.' With some effort, Orton opened the rear door.

It was the stink that hit Holbrooke first. He had largely inured himself to the petrol and burnt-plastic reek coming from the van, but now that it had been opened up the stench became almost unbearable. The windows had not broken in the fire and the fumes had been contained until the first policeman there had prised open the doors.

The acrid smell made him gag and he stepped back, bringing a hand to his mouth. From where he stood, he could see the sickening red-black stains which discoloured the floor of the van. There were similar unsightly marks on the interior metal surfaces as well.

'My guess is that he set it on fire and then left. It's not a professional job. The fire must have looked impressive, but it went out too soon to obliterate all the evidence. A bit of luck for us. We found no tools, but I think it's fairly obvious that this is where he dismembered his victims prior to bagging them and secreting them in the postboxes,' commented Orton who, on the outside at least, appeared unaffected by the grisly, malodorous discovery. 'As you can see, a fairly copious amount of blood has been spilt inside, and I found several marks of a cleaver-type weapon on the floor of the vehicle. It must have been like a slaughterhouse.'

'Another piece of the puzzle yet we seem no closer to catching the bastard.' Having now seen more than enough, Holbrooke signalled to Orton to close the van door.

'You realise we only have a few more days before he strikes again. That's assuming that he sticks to his routine. Still, until he gets himself a new means of transportation, we can hope that this should come as something of a setback. In the interim, I'll see about — '

'Sir!' Inspector Jackson came striding into the garage. 'I've just received a call from the station. I think we might have an important development.'

'What is it?'

'It's to do with that Ray Smith character. You know, the guy's who's been turning up asking all sorts of questions here, there, and everywhere. You thought it was just an alias and it looks like you were right. A woman who works in the post office at Bagley is pretty certain his real name is Montrose. Richard Montrose.'

'How does she know that?'

'Apparently she went to school with him. A bit of a weirdo by all accounts. He fits the bill of a true psycho. He used to live alone with his mother and was always bullied at school. From what she remembers, he was expelled from his previous school for turning up to a biology lesson with a freshly dissected cat.

'Anyway, he'd been in her post office, calling himself Ray Smith and asking about the Postbox Killer a couple of weeks ago. He seemed familiar, but it was only when she dug out an old school photo that it all came back to her.'

Holbrooke nodded. As leads went it was the best he had, for the time being anyway. 'All right. Find out where he lives and get him down to the station. It's time we had a chat with this Mr. Montrose.'

★ ★ ★

Montrose had resigned himself to the fact that there was little more he could do until the Postbox Killer struck again. He was kept busy, having received several new clocks that needed fixing. Yet his mind was always turning to the events at King's funeral, only too well aware that he had come so close to successfully trailing the individual he considered to be the prime suspect. It had only been due to a cruel twist of fate that he was not in possession of the murderer's name and address. As it was, he would just have to remain patient.

It continued to vex him not knowing just how far along the investigation process the police were. Were they close to making an arrest? Or were they, like him, having to wait until victims number five and six turned up?

Nothing was given away in the news bulletins he saw on television or the articles in the tabloids to suggest one thing or another. He wondered whether there had been any copycat killings or missed opportunities, knowing full well that information of that kind would probably not be disclosed to the public.

There came a loud rap at his front door.

Montrose went to his study window and looked down. Two policemen stood there: one tall and uniformed, the other plain-clothed and portly. He cursed under his breath. Heart hammering, he made his way down the stairs and opened the door.

'Mr. Richard Montrose?' asked the detective.

'Yes.'

'I'd like to ask you to come down to the police station. It's in connection with the spate of recent murders. It appears that you've taken quite an interest in them.'

'I didn't realise that was against the law,' replied Montrose defensively.

'There is also the small matter of you assuming a false identity, Mr. Ray Smith. Now then, if you'll just get into the car.'

'So I take it that I'm under arrest. Is that right?' Montrose could see one of his neighbours, who had bent down to retrieve his delivered milk bottles, looking furtively in his direction. No doubt they all suspected him of being the murderer now. Well, let them gloat and gossip for a while. He had made preparations for an event such as this.

★ ★ ★

The interview room at the Oxford police station was slightly less forbidding than that where the ex-wife murderer, Craddock, had been grilled. Still, it was not the most homely of places. Present were Detective Chief Inspector Holbrooke, Inspector Jackson, and Montrose.

After Holbrooke had gone through the legal formalities, he got down to the interrogation. 'You understand that you're not being charged with anything, hence, you have no need to have a lawyer present. You're merely helping us with our enquiries.'

Montrose nodded. 'I understand.'

'Very good.' Holbrooke fixed the horologist with a hard stare. 'Before I begin asking you where you were on certain dates and at certain times, I was hoping you could tell me why exactly you've been carrying out your own investigation into these murders under a false identity.'

'Curiosity mainly,' answered Montrose tersely yet with some degree of truth.

'Curiosity? You know what they say about that, don't you?' Holbrooke sat back in his chair. 'What I'm trying to understand, Mr. Montrose, is why a man like you would devote so much of his time and energy to driving around the area asking so many questions. I dare say there's over a dozen post office workers whom I could call in to successfully identify you.'

'Well, like I said, curiosity.'

'And why the made-up name? What are you trying to hide?'

'I'm not trying to hide anything. I just figured that I would be better keeping some level of mystery in case the murderer himself were to latch on to what I was doing. Call it self-preservation if you like. Besides, I've always liked the name Ray. Don't ask me why.'

'It all sounds like a rather lame explanation.'

'It's the best I can give.'

'Have you at any time ever owned a white van?'

'No,' Montrose answered, filing away that snippet of information. If he played things cleverly, who knew what else he could extract unknowingly from his interrogator?

'Do you have any connection with any of the deceased?'

'Aside from being a slim white male, I don't think so.' Montrose knew that he was pushing things, and he wondered just how far he could take his sarcasm and whether it was wise to do so. He had read about off-the-record use of violence in these interrogation rooms. He would have to rein his answers in a bit, as he did not want to have to limp out of here with a bust lip and several broken ribs.

'You're not being very co-operative. One could be forgiven for thinking that you had something to hide.'

'If that's what you think.' Montrose shrugged his shoulders.

'Maybe you don't realise the seriousness of the situation.'

'Oh, I understand all right. But you

see, I have a perfectly good alibi for the date of the first two murders.' Reaching into his jacket pocket, Montrose drew out his diary.

'Here we are. On both the first and second of April, I was at Birmingham University attending a series of lectures on John Poole's auxiliary compensation with regard to the eight-day box marine chronometer.' There was an almost tangible element of smugness in his voice.

Holbrooke and Jackson exchanged confused glances.

'By profession I'm a horologist. I repair, restore, collect and study clocks and all chronometric devices — whatever age, shape, or design they come in, from the humble egg-timer to the Great Clock of Westminster. One of the time-pieces used as an illustration in the lectures was my own, and I demonstrated it in front of several hundred witnesses. I have a fascination with time, you see. Something which is on my side, but unfortunately not on yours,' Montrose added knowingly.

'What makes you say that?' asked Holbrooke.

'Two reasons.' Perfectly at ease, Montrose sat back and crossed his arms. 'One, I have a cast-iron alibi; and two, you only have a few more days before the killer strikes again.'

'What makes you think that he will?'

'Why stop at four? You have a homicidal maniac out there who will keep killing until he's caught. You know this as well as I do.'

'Do you have anything that we may consider . . . useful?' asked Holbrooke, his eyes narrowing as he pulled thoughtfully at his bottom lip. 'You realise that it is not in your interest to withhold anything which may lead to the capture of the murderer.'

'I hope you're not questioning my civic responsibility, Detective Chief Inspector. I happen to be a perfectly law-abiding member of the public. Yes, I do have an interest in this murderer — which you may find unappealing — but I'm sure there are hundreds, if not thousands, of people similar to me. You have only to go into any public house anywhere in the county, if not the country, and you will be

158

bombarded with all manner of speculation. It seems everyone wants to be an armchair detective these days.'

'Be that as it may, your interest in this has gone a little too far for my liking.' Holbrooke scribbled down something on a piece of paper and handed it over to Jackson. On it he had written: apply for a search warrant.

'So arrest me. Throw me in a police cell. Then, when some time on the third of June two more bodies are found dismembered in postboxes, you can let me out. In the meantime, you can of course come round and search my house. But you won't find any concealed basements filled with blood-soaked saws or axes, of that I can assure you,' said Montrose, having already cottoned on to the idea that Holbrooke would want to have a good rummage around his property.

'What you will find is the home of a law-abiding bachelor. Yes, I freely admit to possessing quite a lot of literature on violent crime; and if that offends you I offer no apology. You will also find my workshop wherein I keep and work on my not-insubstantial collection of antique time-telling devices. So you see, Detective Chief Inspector, you have nothing on me. Nothing at all.'

Holbrooke knew the other had just spoken the truth. The man was odd, creepy almost; but that aside, his use of a fake identity was about the only thing he could pin on him at the moment. He would keep hold of him until the alibi had checked out, but that would only take a few phone calls.

In addition, it was questionable whether a search of the Montrose residence was necessary. He was sure that the judge would approve it, as all of them were under such pressure to make progress; but Montrose had not seemed at all worried by the prospect. It appeared that this lead, which had seemed so promising at the time, would result in yet another dead end.

★　★　★

The search warrant was granted after the briefest of delays. The last thing anyone in the justice system wanted was for another opportunity to catch the Postbox Killer to slip through their fingers, knowing full well the questions which would be asked if they failed to act.

Consequently, at around two o'clock in the afternoon, a small team of policemen carried out a thorough search of the house in which the horologist lived. Inquisitive neighbours gazed on the proceedings surreptitiously from behind venetian blinds or suddenly decided now was the time to mow the lawn and peer over the fence.

Montrose himself was there, although he had been told to stay outside in the garden at all times. For the past fifteen minutes he had been talking quite animatedly to an elderly, affable and slightly avuncular constable who had been instructed to keep an eye on him.

'So you see,' Montrose expounded, 'there are many similarities between how Christie operated and the murders attributed to the Victorian killer, Doctor Thomas Cream. In addition, both had attempted to pin the crime on another. However, it is for something that is reported to have happened during the last few seconds of his life that Cream is perhaps best remembered. Sentenced to hang for the murder of a twenty-seven-year-old prostitute, he allegedly stood calm and collected at the gallows at Newgate prison. Then, quite suddenly, just as he was about to drop, he is said to have uttered: 'I am Jack'.'

'Jack? As in Jack the Ripper?' The police constable asked excitedly, having a passing interest in Ripperology.

'The one and only.' Montrose heard a crash from inside his house. It sounded as though a shelf full of plates had hit the floor. 'I take it I'll be fully compensated for any damage caused?'

'Why certainly.'

'And they know that all the items in my workshop have to be treated very, very carefully? Some of the pieces in there are irreplaceable.'

'Don't you worry, Mr. Montrose.' The police constable obviously shared the other's love of death and those who dealt it, for he immediately returned to their topic of discussion: 'Do you think they'll ever establish who the real Jack the Ripper was? I've read a number of stories on the subject. Some reckon he was involved with the Masons and some say he was a member of the Royal Family.'

'The Masonic connection — ' Montrose winced upon hearing a further crash. 'What the hell are they doing in there? Wrecking the place?'

'As I said, don't you worry about it. All will be made right as rain before we leave. You have my word on that.'

'Well they're certainly taking their time.' Montrose looked at his wristwatch. 'Have you any idea how much longer this is going to go on for?'

'As long as it takes, I'm afraid. You should know that, with all your expertise on crime. We have to go over everything with a fine-toothed comb. Evidence collection — it's that which forms the backbone to our detection methods.'

Montrose sighed resignedly. He looked skywards, noting the grey clouds that were beginning to mar the blue sky. The first few spits of rain started to fall on his upturned face.

'Now then, you were talking about the Masons. I've always wondered — ' The police constable stopped on seeing his colleagues exit the house, some carrying box files and folders. He turned to Montrose. 'Looks like it's all over.'

Inspector Jackson was the last to leave. He strode across the lawn towards Montrose.

'All right, you're free to go back inside. We've taken into our keeping some of your documents as well as your map for further examination. Don't go anywhere without informing us, and in future take my advice and stay well clear of this investigation. Believe me, you don't want to get on the wrong side of Holbrooke if he gets fired up . . . or me for that matter. So consider this a warning if you like. Next time we'll think of something to bang you away for.'

★ ★ ★

'It goes without saying that the guy's a freak,' commented Jackson. 'Some of the books he had were stomach-churning.

I've got a few of Orton's lab rats going through them now, but in all honesty I don't think there's anything there. Just a macabre obsession.'

Detective Chief Inspector Holbrooke sat behind his desk and took a drink from his coffee cup. 'From what you've seen, do you think it merits some level of surveillance?'

His face creasing, Jackson thought about it for a moment. 'We could, but maybe we'd be better off getting as many bobbies as we can on the beat. You mentioned drafting in some support from the neighbouring forces. Any success there?'

'Yes. We've got two divisions coming in from Bedfordshire and one from Hampshire. In addition all leave has been cancelled. The idea is to make it nigh on impossible for the killer to gain access to any postbox in the area. We can't cover the whole region and there are bound to be gaps, but hopefully it will make the bastard think twice before he strikes again.

'There's also going to be news coverage

warning the public not to venture out alone unless it is deemed an emergency. Whether people will pay any attention to it I don't know, but it should help.' Holbrooke irritably ran his fingers through his thinning hair. 'The truth is that we're going to have to wait for the killer to mess up again, like he did with Craven. I've been wondering if we should actually put out some officers as bait. Set them walking along byways with another man concealed nearby as backup.'

'It might work, but the resources you'd need for that would be phenomenal.'

'I'm going to put it to the chief superintendent anyway. If we got it right then it would mean stopping this bastard before he kills again, rather than trying to catch him disposing of a body.' Holbrooke was warming to his idea.

'If we can call in some of the extra officers a day early we could get maybe a dozen teams together: one thin man to be the lure, with a beefier one ready to reel the fish in. If the public warning works, then the only available victims will be us.'

Montrose surveyed his home with annoyance. The police had done a decent job of tidying up after themselves, but the evidence of the interference was everywhere. He was punctilious about order, and everything from his sofa cushions to his few ornaments were kept in exactly the same position week in, week out. Now it was all different and would take him hours to sort out.

Walking upstairs to his workshop, he was relieved to see all his precious clocks were safe and had in fact hardly been touched, although his tools had been more thoroughly examined.

The change to his crime files, however, was more glaring. All of his cuttings about the killings had been taken, as had the copious notes he had made. He cursed under his breath. At least there was nothing incriminating in them that could lead to more questioning.

He was fortunate that he had not written anything down about his unsuccessful pursuit of the suspect from King's funeral. It was also extremely lucky that he had been at the Birmingham University Clock Conference in April, or he might well have been arrested by now.

It was obvious that the police were getting desperate, searching for a scapegoat, and he would not have put it past them to frame him for the murders.

He looked around his workshop and gratefully patted the case of the clock he had taken to Birmingham. That had been a stroke of luck and no mistake. Sitting down, he wondered if he should take Inspector Jackson's advice and steer clear of it all. The sound of the various clocks seem to echo his indecision, vacillating between 'yes' and 'no' with each tick.

8

Friday, the second day of June, dawned bright and warm; yet, as far as Montrose was concerned, there was a portentous tension in the air — a strange expectant quality that hovered menacingly over him.

With some trepidation, he went to his bedroom window and pulled back the curtain. Looking out, he quite suddenly felt nervous, ill at ease. It was as if something terrible was about to happen and there was nothing he or anybody else could do to prevent it.

There was a momentary twitch of fear along the muscles of his back, which prompted him to turn around as though half-expecting to see some dark-coated stranger framed in the doorway or for the door to his wardrobe to slowly swing open, revealing some murderous bogey-man. There was no one there, but the flash of his own reflection in a mirror startled him.

He got dressed and went downstairs to make breakfast, battling not to succumb to the paranoiac sense of dread that threatened to take possession of him.

Yes, today was the day when the killer would quite probably strike again — but why did he have this overwhelming suspicion that he was going to be targeted? It made no sense whatsoever. Why on earth did his troubled mind cling to that possibility? For some reason, he believed there was a certain inevitability that he would be victim number five.

Was that why he had been so driven to find the murderer in the first place?

He felt like screaming. Why was he thinking like this? The odds against him being murdered, chopped up and binned in a pillar box were surely astronomical.

Besides, he would make damn sure he would stay in tonight. To hell with any idea of going out and stalking the murderer. He would leave that to the police. It was their job, after all. Let them sort it out.

Running the back of his hand over his forehead, he noticed that there was a chill dampness there. Desperately, he clamped his teeth tightly together and forced himself to breathe slowly. He had to get a grip on his senses and start thinking clearly, otherwise he would surely go mad.

The minutes ticked by slowly as he grappled with his own morbid thoughts and delusions, knowing at the back of his mind that this was something he would never relinquish interest in. Things had gone too far now. Way too far.

* * *

The police presence that began to build up from late morning that day was unprecedented, as a veritable army of uniformed officers took their positions in many of the small rural villages. A few roadblocks were established, but after these were found to be nothing but a major inconvenience they were taken down. Now and then a low-flying police helicopter circled overhead.

By around two o'clock, the temperature had soared. Detective Chief Inspector

Holbrooke was sweating in his office, co-ordinating the reports as they came in. He had managed to put together fourteen two-man 'bait' teams that had been assigned to back roads across the county. Each was in radio contact with a central hub, and so far all was quiet. It was a long shot that one of them would be targeted by the killer, especially in broad daylight, but Holbrooke's superiors had agreed that it was well worth trying. The authorities had taken so much criticism over the handling of this investigation that they were desperate to cover their own backs if indeed the killer did strike again.

Holbrooke tried to imagine what might be going on inside the killer's head. Would he be spooked by the visible police presence and change his tactics, or would he see it as a challenge? The possibility that the murderer would just stop and give up his homicidal urges was not on the cards. Someone who killed for personal gain might stop when their aim had been achieved. But this man had no such motive as far as they could tell. The best the police could come up with was that the killer derived satisfaction from the murders, and with that motivation there seemed no reason why he would not continue.

It was at times like this that Holbrooke remembered the single most important lesson he had ever learned in his training: the fact that the police service only worked because most of society allowed it to. The percentage of officers to members of the public was tiny — far too few for it to be possible to ensure the rule of law through force alone. The system relied on the threat of capture more than most people realised. The papers and many of the general public were castigating the police for not having miraculously tracked the killer to his lair, assuming laziness or stupidity was the reason for the delay. But it was impossible to interview everyone; to keep everywhere under surveillance.

If the Postbox Killer continued to be careful and clever, he might never be caught.

★   ★   ★

It was building up to be an excellent night for a murder . . . or two: a humid, sticky night with thunder creeping up from the south.

It was a little past ten when Montrose got up from his worn sofa and switched off the television. There had been countless news reports warning people to stay inside if at all possible, and renewed pleas for anyone with information to contact the police, but no mention of any further killings that evening. Not that that was of much surprise, for the victims tended not to be found until the next day.

Having now overcome the fear that had gripped him earlier, Montrose's curiosity was once more aroused. It was almost as if he wanted to be a part of the murders — neither as an accomplice nor as a direct witness, but as one who could appreciate the way in which it was done.

In this manner, he likened himself to an art lover; one who admired the creation of something that, although not always aesthetically beautiful, required skill and vision and was in some way unique. Which of course made the murderer an artist; one who painted his subjects on a canvas in strokes of blood red.

He needed to understand the means, and more importantly the mentality, behind the killer. It would be disastrous if tonight would prove to be the murderer's last. His luck was bound to run out some time, and considering the numbers arrayed against him . . .

Montrose found himself reflecting on whether or not the murderer would adopt a new strategy in order to satiate his homicidal passions. Would he, for example, postpone his campaign of terror to another night, thus breaking his own code, or would he be brave and take a chance? If he could somehow pull off a fifth or even a sixth murder then it would be a major coup for him — and an immense catastrophe for the police, for it would highlight their ineptitude. It would be some achievement if the killer could do it. Praiseworthy almost.

The thought that right now, at this very moment in time, the killer could be lying in wait, ready to pounce, thrilled Montrose. It was going to be hard to get to sleep but he decided there was no point in staying up. Even if something happened, it would not reach the television news channels or radio stations until tomorrow. Like a child awaiting Christmas Day, the best thing he could do was to go to bed and be ready to act in the morning. He shut up the house, took his radio upstairs and, despite his excitement, was asleep by eleven o'clock.

★　★　★

It might have been a creaky floorboard that made Montrose wake up a short time after he had fallen asleep, or perhaps an owl hooting nearby; but more likely it was an animal instinct that he was no longer alone. Whatever the reason, he opened his eyes and scanned the dark room.

His blood froze in his veins when he saw the shadowy figure leaning against his bedroom door. Overcoming a momentary paralysis, Montrose spoke. 'Who are you?' He tried to say it forcefully, but his voice cracked and sounded weak and scared.

'You tell me,' the man answered, a hint

176

of mockery in his tone.

Montrose could not see well in the darkened room, but he had a horrible certainty that he did know who the stranger must be. He swallowed a lump in his throat and hoped his voice would sound less pathetic this time. 'You're the Postbox Killer, aren't you?'

'Correct, although most people — those who know me better — call me Michael Sutherland.'

Montrose felt sick at the words. He had been longing to put a name to the killer, but not like this. He knew that the prospect of getting out of this alive had just become even more remote, as murderers generally only revealed themselves if the listener was not long for this world. His mind was in overdrive, looking for a way out of the nightmare. That made him think for the briefest of moments if this was just a bad dream; a figment of his troubled imagination conjured up by his unhealthy obsession.

He bit his bottom lip, feeling the pain register, knowing that this was no phantom standing before him.

'How . . . how did you find me?' he asked, forcing the words out.

'It wasn't difficult. I saw you following me back from the funeral of Number Four, and I remembered you had been hanging around at Number Three's send-off too. I know Farthingswell like the back of my hand and it was easy to take a side road and end up behind you. I don't think you looked in your mirror even once; you were so busy looking ahead, trying to find me.

'Then you hurried home and I began to get interested in Mr. Richard Montrose.' Sutherland turned on a torch, shining it directly in Montrose's face. 'Get dressed. We're going for a walk.'

Blinking in the sudden light, Montrose had to fight against the panic that was threatening to overcome him. 'You . . . you must be joking.'

Sutherland drew a heavy revolver from his jacket. 'No joke. Get dressed!' he ordered.

Reluctantly, Montrose got out of bed and hastily pulled on the clothes he had been wearing during the day, putting the trousers on over his pyjamas. He did not have a weapon of any kind in the house, except for some kitchen knives, and he could not think of a way to get to them.

'Right. Now we're going downstairs, you first.' Sutherland shone the torch on the floor and gestured with the gun.

Edging to the bedroom door, Montrose got a better view of the man and saw that he was wearing a rather obvious black wig and fake moustache, but he recognised the piercing, dark eyes and prominent cheekbones. There were no lines on his face and he could not have been more than about thirty, but his expression was the coldest the horologist had ever seen.

Despite his fear, he found himself growing curious again. Here he was, actually in the presence of one of the country's most successful killers. If he was clever enough and very lucky, he might survive the encounter and get the answers he craved.

They walked down the stairs and towards the back door, which Montrose noticed had a neat circle of glass missing from one of its panels. Stepping out of the house, he reflected that it would have been handy if he had left a spade or something in the garden; but he always tidied away meticulously.

Seeing a light on in a neighbour's bedroom window, he wondered about screaming for help, but knew that would only hasten his demise. He expected Sutherland to direct him to the street, but was surprised when he was steered towards the fields at the back of his house. There was a footpath there that he had seldom been along.

There was a far-off flash of lightning. Distant thunder rumbled ominously.

'Where are we going?' Montrose asked.
'Not far.'

Montrose walked on, slowly, not knowing whether he should try and make a break for it. With luck, he might be able to dash into the thicker shadows that now crowded in around them.

A light drizzle began to fall, becoming steadily heavier.

'Any sudden moves and you're a dead man.'

Montrose gulped nervously. It was as though his captor had read his mind.

'We keep going until we get to the gate. We then take a left turn. Follow the path for a couple of hundred yards until you reach the old barn.'

'Okay.'

'And like I said, no funny business. Believe me, I won't hesitate to shoot you.'

Now that they were a sufficient distance away from the houses, Sutherland began to talk more. 'No doubt you're wondering why I haven't killed you yet.'

'The thought had crossed my mind,' replied Montrose, looking back over his shoulder.

'I've found out that you're not a cop, so why the interest in me, and who else knows about me? That's the important thing. Tell me what I want to know and no harm will come to you, I assure you.'

Montrose knew that Sutherland's words lacked sincerity. He was sure that he was being led somewhere quiet and secluded so that the murderer could finish him off. Had he been thinking rationally, he might have fabricated some story that his death or disappearance would result in the immediate revelation of the killer's identity. However, with the spectre of imminent death hanging over him he only managed to say: 'I'm just interested in murders. That's all.'

'Really? So not me in particular?'

'No.'

'I'm disappointed,' commented the killer, his words devoid of emotion. 'We're getting near the gate. Turn left.'

Montrose pushed open the gate and set out along a new path. This one was wider and had at one time or another been a farm track. He had been out here before and knew that it led to a long-abandoned silage barn — a perfect place to kill someone.

He stumbled several times on the track and tried not to think of himself as a condemned man walking to his death. There seemed no opportunity yet to act, but he had so many questions that he could not keep quiet.

'Why postboxes?' he blurted out. 'And the date — the second of the month?'

'Both William's suggestions.'

'William?'

'You'll meet him soon enough.'

'And why go to these lengths in the

first place?' Montrose felt he was pushing his luck, but he had to ask.

'You're persistent, aren't you? Well, you answer a few of my questions and I might answer yours.'

The rain was falling heavily now and Montrose's shirt was soaked through. His hair hung damply on his forehead.

'When the police raided your house, was there anything that would lead them to me?' Sutherland demanded.

'You saw that?' Montrose asked in surprise.

'I moved my base of operations over here after I found you. I'd got rid of my van before that anyway, so I needed to find somewhere quiet to do my work. The arrival of four police cars just a stone's throw away naturally caught my attention. So, did you write anything down or take any pictures that would lead them to me?'

Montrose paused, unsure whether to tell the truth or not. Would it help him to lie? He decided that Sutherland was intending to kill him regardless, so he might as well be truthful.

'I'd be surprised if they can make anything of my notes. I didn't know your name or where you lived, and I had no photographs. I didn't tell them about seeing you at the funerals either.'

'Why not? They were obviously suspicious of you.'

'I didn't want them to find you,' Montrose answered, panting slightly as the strain of the walk, the weather, and the situation began to take its toll.

'And why was that?' Sutherland asked, his voice betraying a hint of confusion. They were coming out into a desolate farmyard and he motioned his prisoner to the metal doors of the barn.

'I wanted to know all about you for myself, not to tell, just to know.' As he finally explained his motivation to someone, Montrose realised just what had been driving him on. 'I didn't want to catch you. I wanted to see how far you could get, and for me to be the only one who knew who you were.'

Sutherland pushed open the door to the barn and motioned with the gun for his captive to enter. 'Stay there,' he ordered and pulled the door shut.

It was darker inside the barn but Montrose could make out the shape of a car that had been hidden inside. There was a lingering mixture of unsavoury farmyard smells in the air: cow dung, decaying straw, swill long ago gone bad.

Sutherland opened the car door, reached inside and started the engine. The headlights were switched on and Montrose blinked, momentarily blinded. Rubbing his eyes, he gasped with horror upon seeing, over to one corner, a pile of bloody sheets.

Sutherland noticed Montrose's reaction. 'Don't worry, they're empty. I've already done Number Five. You'd think people would pay attention to the news, but thankfully not everyone does. The cops think they've got all the postboxes covered, but I know every single one, and I slipped past them easily enough.' He stepped away from his car, his gun still pointing unwaveringly at Montrose. He walked closer and regarded him curiously.

'You wanted to see how many murders I could get away with? Either you're lying or you're sicker than I am!' He laughed harshly. 'You want to know why post-boxes? Well, this is why. Have a look in the car.'

Keeping his eyes on Sutherland, Montrose warily approached the car. The interior was in shadowy darkness, but he could just discern a figure seated in the back seat.

'Have a closer look.' Sutherland shone his torch over.

Propped upright in the seat was a rotting corpse dressed in the remnants of a black, tattered, funereal suit. The yellowy-green skin was pulled tautly over the skull, the eyes sunken holes.

'This is William, my brother and the architect of all my crimes,' Sutherland announced.

Montrose stared in horror at the corpse. Never had he imagined anything like this. This bordered on the exploits of Ed Gein.

'William was killed before we could carry out his plans but he never let me down. He's talked to me every day since I brought him back up.'

'Up?' Montrose managed to croak. Anyone in their right mind would have tried to flee by now, even if it meant taking a bullet in the back, but his fascination was almost as strong as his fear.

'Six feet up, to be precise. He was calling to me for years, telling me to come and get him.' Sutherland looked at his long-dead brother with something akin to reverence. 'It took time for me to hear him properly.'

'You . . . you said it was William's idea to use the postboxes?' Montrose asked. The police would have simply dismissed Sutherland as insane, but there must have been a reason for the madness to manifest in this extraordinary fashion.

'Poetic justice, seeing as he never had any other kind,' Sutherland said, his voice cold. 'William got knocked down and killed by a van, a postal van, that ran into and over him. He was fifteen and he bled to death on the road. The driver had been speeding. He got off with a pitiful sentence and then vanished.' Sutherland began to pace the floor.

'For ten years I tried to find the bastard, and when I did I ran him over, several times. I knew William would help me then. It all came back to me, all his ideas.' He turned and looked piercingly at Montrose. 'You know a lot about crime. So did he. When he was a kid he wanted to be a detective, but by the time he'd grown up and seen a little more of how bad the world is, his desire changed to becoming the perfect killer.'

Montrose nodded. 'In some ways I can relate to that,' he said. Sutherland was showing less control now and there could be a chance to turn the tables on him. However enthralled he was by the story, and he truly was, he would prefer to end this night alive.

'It was William's theory that the reason murderers got caught was that they had a connection to the victim. If you just picked complete strangers and were clever about it, you could be unstoppable. I've proved him right. Four murders so far, two more tonight; one for William, one for me. Which brings me to you, Number Six.'

Menacingly, Sutherland began advancing forward. He raised the gun.

There was nothing else for it. Montrose spun on his heel and made a dash for the exit. He heard a curse and then something hard hit him between the shoulder blades, undoubtedly the gun which he assumed had either jammed or had never been loaded in the first place. He yanked hard on the metal door, then he was outside.

A flash of lightning rent the murk asunder. The rain was pouring down now, soaking everything in its miserable deluge.

Montrose slipped in the mud. Frantically, he scrambled to his feet.

Sutherland was there, rearing over him. Snarling insanely, he swung down with a hammer, striking Montrose a glancing blow on the shoulder.

The heavy tool came down a second time.

Montrose caught the killer's wrist. With his other hand, he made a grab at Sutherland's throat. He pushed fiercely as he wrestled to gain control of the blunt weapon, fear lending him strength.

Slickly, his fingers slipped up his assailant's neck, over his jaw, to his face. He made his hand claw-like, digging his nails into the wet flesh and drawing blood.

With a heave, Sutherland threw Montrose clear but in so doing lost his hold on the hammer. His face was now a rain-soaked mess, muddy and blood-smeared. His black wig had been dragged to one side, revealing his cropped blond hair beneath.

Retrieving the fallen hammer, Montrose held it threateningly. 'Get away from me!' he shouted. A second later a terrific crack of thunder sounded directly overhead. 'Get away or so help me, I'll — '

Sutherland leapt forward.

Montrose swung out. The hammer smote the side of the murderer's head with a bone-jarring crunch.

Sutherland staggered back. He shook spasmodically for a moment and then his dark eyes glazed over and his knees buckled beneath him. He gazed pathetically, sightlessly, and then fell face first in the mud, dead.

For a long moment, Montrose looked

down at the body at his feet. He dared not move, not knowing whether Sutherland was only stunned or if he had indeed killed him. Then, as the seconds turned to minutes, and the rain and mud gurgled around the prone man, he knew that he himself was a murderer.

Yes, it was in self-defence, but he had still intentionally killed another human being. The realisation was not particularly unpleasant, but he still had the problem of how to get away with it. He stood there, utterly soaked. Then a thought came to him. Everything he needed was in the barn — the tools, the sheet, the car.

The Aldingham Estate was not too far away . . . and it had a particularly interesting pillar box.

★ ★ ★

The thunder of the previous night had cleared the air and June the third promised to be sunny and dry.

Orton opened the door to the police car that had just pulled into the layby on the Aldingham Estate, nine miles from

Long Gallop where two months earlier the Postbox Killer had first gained notoriety. 'You're not going to believe this, James. I thought I'd seen everything, but . . . '

'What do you — ' Holbrooke stopped in mid-sentence and, from his car seat, stared disbelievingly at the sight before him.

The estate was big enough to have rated a double pillar box: one slot for first-class and one for second. The single large door was open and he could see that the left-hand side of the cavity held a naked, dismembered body.

However, on the right hand-side was a horribly withered, long-dead corpse wearing a thick bushy moustache and a black wig.

Death After Death

'Darling, whatever's the matter? You look awful.'

Anthony Harris rubbed at his blood-shot eyes and tried to focus on his wife, who was seated at the kitchen table. This was the third morning that week he had woken up screaming. He now stood wobbling slightly, his face pale and sickly-looking. His hair was wild and he was still dressed in his pyjamas. He cursed as a bare foot came down painfully on a discarded plastic toy.

One-year-old Alfie Harris let out a bleat of laughter from where he sat next to his mother and waved his arms, accidentally knocking over a bottle of milk.

'Are you — ' Pauline Harris got to her feet.

'Oh my God!' Unsteadily, Harris stumbled forward and managed to reach a chair. Using the table as a support, he sank down, his head in his hands. He was shaking noticeably. Twisting his face, he screwed up his eyes momentarily as if trying to shut out the memory of something that was too horrible to contemplate. Then he shook his head and took a tight grip on himself.

'What is it?' Pauline moved towards him, placing a comforting arm around his shoulder. 'Was it another bad dream?'

For a moment Harris was silent. He seemed to be suffering from one of the worst hangovers imaginable. He began tugging gently at his ruffled hair. 'That was the worst so far. It was . . . horrible.'

'Let me get you a coffee.' Pauline prepared to move away.

'It was so real. So bloody real . . . with an emphasis on the bloody. It was as though I was actually there. I feel as though — ' Harris quickly reached out for his wife's now-empty cereal bowl and threw up into it. A cold shiver went through his entire body and he began to shake convulsively. Wiping strands of sick and spit from his quivering lips, he slumped against the table, his breath

196

coming out in great wracking heaves.

'I'll phone Doctor Yates.'

Now that he had been sick, Harris felt marginally better. 'No . . . that won't be necessary. Besides, I've an appointment with him this afternoon.'

He leaned back in his chair and began to regulate his breathing. The sight and smell of his fresh vomit in the bowl almost triggered a second bout of nausea but he managed to force it down. 'I'll have that coffee though. Black and extra strong.'

'Sure.' Pauline gathered up the bowl and made for the sink. After disposing of the vomit and rinsing clean the bowl, she began boiling the kettle.

Harris tried his best to smile at his son but succeeded only in a grimace. He knew he had to keep down the horrible images that had plagued him in the last few minutes before waking. The very thought of the vileness that his subconscious had conjured in his brain sent a further jolt through his body. He felt like tilting his head back and screaming to the ceiling. For in his nightmare he had seen himself looking down on his own torn-apart body. His broken, severed limbs lay scattered around his blood-drenched torso and yet he could see he was still alive, his mouth working madly, yelling insanely, his eyes filled with blood and terror.

'Will you be all right going to work this morning?' Pauline asked, pouring his drink. She came over and rested the steaming cup by her husband's elbow.

'Yes. I think so. Besides, it's only a half day.' Harris worked as a technician at a large industrial research centre some ten miles away. 'I'll finish this drink, then I'll go and have a shower.'

'Do you feel up to having any breakfast?'

'Just some toast.' Harris sipped at his coffee. He was trying to put things into perspective; to come to terms with his horrendous vision and to deal with the insanity of what he had witnessed some half an hour previously. It was just a dream — a particularly vivid and nasty dream, but a dream nonetheless. He pinched his hand, feeling the pain register, ensuring to himself that this was reality. It had been unlike anything he had . . . He stopped himself. There had been something once, something similar. But that had been long ago. Very long ago.

A fresh bout of confusion and madness threatened to seize him as he sought to untwine the dark vines now growing in his mind.

'Here's your — ' Pauline stopped, seeing the ghastly look on her husband's deathly pale face. 'I'm going to phone Doctor Yates right away.' She put down the plate, on which were four slices of buttered toast and raspberry jam, and made for the hall.

'No!' Harris looked up. 'I'll be all right. Honestly. All I need is — ' The sight of the lumpy dark-red jam almost triggered another bout of sickness. He stared at the sticky preserve, half-expecting it to suddenly liquefy and seep over the plate. He turned away quickly. Gulping, he staggered like a cripple to his feet.

'Take my advice and go back to bed. I'll phone your boss and say you won't be in.'

'I have to go in today. There's an important job on this morning.'

'Don't be a fool, Anthony! You're sick. Anyone can see that. I'm sure that Mr. Burgess will be very understanding. It's not as though you've ever missed a day before.'

'I . . . I'm feeling better already.' It was a lie but Harris knew he had to say something. It was imperative that he went to work today. 'Maybe I'll feel better after a quick shower.' Ignoring his wife's protestations, he somehow made his way out of the kitchen and climbed the stairs to the bathroom.

★　★　★

Forty minutes later, after Harris had showered, dressed and drunk two more strong coffees, he got in his car, ready to go to work.

It was a fine morning, the bright early-spring sunlight warm and pleasant. He switched on the car engine and put it into reverse, then backed out of the drive and turned on to the main road.

Mercifully, he was now genuinely feeling better. Now that the initial shock was fading, dissolving from his mind, he felt that he could properly tackle the day ahead. He focused on driving, pleased to have something grounding to divert his troubled mind. The details of the nightmare were now hazy; little interconnected pieces of horror that were gradually evaporating — a troubling smoke that was becoming a mist. If he managed to stop thinking about it, perhaps it would soon vanish completely. In time, it might become something he could laugh at.

He settled back in his seat. Houses flashed past as he stepped on the accelerator. Soon he was out in the countryside. He turned on the car radio. It was tuned to a classical music station and some loud operatic piece, filled with gusto and bravura, blasted forth. It was not anything he had ever heard before but it was rousing stuff all the same.

The music finished in time for the eight o'clock news. After the broadcaster had introduced himself he went straight into the main story: 'Police were this morning called to an address in Croydon, where they discovered the dismembered body of a man. The butchered remains of forty-four-year-old Anthony Harris were found . . . '

A shockwave blasted through Harris's mind. His hands left the steering wheel and the car swerved dangerously. Thoughts raged through his brain. Fear was a black cloud about him, choking and suffocating, stifling his breath and threatening to stop the thudding of his heart. At the last moment he regained control of the car and steered it back from disaster. Through the insanity, he managed to take in the closing news item.

' . . . the deceased's wife, thirty-five-year-old Pauline Harris, has been taken into custody. The police are not looking for anyone else in connection with the grisly murder. In other news, the supermarket giant . . . '

Heart thumping, Harris switched the radio off and brought the car to a stop. He sat there gazing absently through the windscreen, his fingertips gently patting his damp forehead. His brain was rambling, descending through a veritable host of dark and senseless possibilities, trying to pull an answer from the irrational thoughts and half-formed ideas that ran chaotically through his mind.

Was he on the verge of going insane?

His surroundings darkened as clouds gusted in from the north. Everything about him was suddenly ominous, filled with a dread that was impossible to overcome. It was as though dark claws were reaching for him, tearing into his psyche, attempting to rip his very being to pieces.

'No!' he screamed, bringing his fists down heavily on the dashboard. 'It can't be!' He looked up at his reflection in the rear-view mirror, and for a second he was convinced that the man who looked back at him from the reflective surface was someone other than he. Then his familiar visage reappeared. There was a haunted look in his eyes and perspiration sheened his skin.

There came a sudden rap on the side window.

Harris jumped in his seat. He turned and saw a young police constable gazing in at him. He wound down the window.

'Good morning, sir. I take it everything's all right?'

Harris nodded. It was the best he could do at the moment.

'I must say your driving back there was a little erratic. You're very lucky there was no oncoming traffic when you veered across the road.'

'I . . . I had a fright. That's all,' replied Harris.

'A fright?'

'Yes . . . I've not been sleeping too well of late and I . . . ' Harris paused. 'Do I look all right to you?

The police constable stood confused. 'Why . . . yes.'

So at least I'm not lying chopped up in a black body bag in the back of an ambulance on the way to the morgue. Harris let out a long sigh of relief. 'Well, I do apologise for my driving back there, constable. I assure you it won't happen again. A momentary lapse, that's all.'

'Very good. Seeing as there was no

harm done, I suppose I'll let you off this time, but please be more careful in future.' Satisfied, the police constable prepared to move off.

'There hasn't been anything major reported in town this morning, has there?' Harris asked. 'No, well, murders or anything?'

'Not that I'm aware of, sir.' The policeman looked at him curiously. 'Why do you ask?' There was a touch of suspicion in his tone.

'I thought I heard something on the radio. That's all.' Harris smiled and tried to look more normal than he felt. 'Maybe it was somewhere else. Well, if it's all right with you, constable, I'd best be getting to work, and I can assure you I'll take it more carefully.'

* * *

That news item had been nothing more than his feverish imagination playing tricks on him, he tried to convince himself as he pulled into the research centre. He drove up to the main checkpoint and fumbled with his security pass. Slowly the barrier was raised and he turned off the avenue, heading for the staff car park.

It was then, just as he was about to park the car, that he felt a peculiar tingling in his wrists. It was as though a hundred hot little needles were pricking into his skin. He stopped the car in a parking bay and rolled up his sleeves, alarmed to see that both forearms, from about halfway down to the wrists, were now covered with a mysterious blue-red weal. Fear surged through his brain as he stared in puzzlement and horror, not knowing just what had happened. Was it some kind of allergic reaction? He felt like screaming. 'What the hell?' he asked himself as, removing his wristwatch, he began to rub at the strange marks in the vain hope that he could wipe them away.

Things were now becoming very sore. There was a tightening sensation and he began to lose all feeling in his hands. He tried to flex his fingers but found it excruciating.

Biting down his pain, and using his

shoulder and his elbow, Harris somehow managed to open the car door. He had no sooner clambered out when he felt his arms being raised as though they were being pulled by invisible ropes. He no longer had any control over his own body. Matters were made worse when he felt a similar sensation around his ankles. There was an agonising squeezing.

For a fleeting second he was lifted a couple of inches off the ground.

A car door slammed shut nearby.

Harris's feet landed back on the tarmac.

'Morning, Anthony!' called out a deep voice. 'I take it you're all set for the testing of the new — ' Edward Burgess, the chief director of the site and Harris's boss, came striding forward, fixing his glasses to his face. 'Are you feeling all right? You look a little peaky, if you don't mind me saying.'

Harris looked worse than peaky; he looked downright awful, but at least he was back on the ground and the pain in his wrists and ankles had all but vanished. The marks on his arms were still plainly visible. They were now beginning to turn an ugly, bruised blue-black.

'There's a nasty bug going around just now.' With no further talk, Burgess started for the main buildings.

Harris watched him go. Had the man not seen what had just happened? And as for the discolouration on his arms — surely he would have noticed.

Now that the pain had finally gone, he found himself getting dazedly back into his car. Taking in some deep breaths, he tried to regain some element of composure. As a scientist, he had always sought to explain the world about him in a clinical, logical manner. Yet he knew that there was something seriously wrong with him. For even if he had just imagined all that had happened to him so far this morning, there was no denying the reality of the marks on his arms. They stood out livid and stark.

Yet his boss had failed to see them.

He examined them again. He ran his fingertips over the wounds, feeling the rough abrasions on the damaged skin. If this was all some kind of delusion, perhaps brought on by a sickened mind, then why were they tangible?

Confused, he opened the car door, stuck a trousered leg out, and rolled up the hemline, not particularly surprised to see the same red raw weal just above his sock.

That was it. Coming swiftly to the conclusion that he had to seek professional help, Harris pulled his leg back inside, slammed the car door and drove off. His determination to get to work seemed ludicrous to him now. His appointment with Doctor Yates was scheduled for later that afternoon, but surely what he was experiencing called for immediate assistance.

A disturbing sensation of impending disaster began to take hold of him, stirring deep in the vaults of his mind. There had been times in the past when a kind of warning bell had rung, alerting him to danger long before it actually materialised, and he knew from instinct never to ignore it. The thought made him grip the steering wheel tighter, almost convulsively, his muscles tautening themselves of their own volition.

With a conscious mental effort, he forced himself to think clearly. He had to put things into some kind of perspective. He was undoubtedly sick; suffering from some mental disorder. The sooner he could be diagnosed by an expert and given proper medication, the better.

The traffic up ahead had slowed down. A tailback had formed and Harris could see the cause — a slow-moving tractor. However, he failed to notice the sign on the verge informing motorists of the hedge-trimming taking place five hundred yards ahead.

The country road was narrow and full of hidden twists and turns that made overtaking treacherous. Seizing their opportunity, the two cars ahead of him pulled out and made the manoeuvre, each nipping back into the lane before a sudden bend.

Harris edged his car forward so that he was now directly behind the tractor. He could see the mud being kicked up by its huge deep-treaded tyres, and even with the windows down he could smell the cow dung it emitted. Small clouds of black, noxious exhaust fumes belched out.

Tattered fragments of the nightmare were returning unbidden and unwelcome to Harris's memory. Terror raced through his body and there was a dull throbbing at the back of his temples, behind his eyes. Wiping a sheen of damp sweat from his forehead, he shifted the car to the right slightly, gauging the road ahead, wondering if he could overtake.

There were no turn-offs and he knew that in all likelihood he would be behind this frustratingly slow-moving vehicle for a good time, for its driver showed no sign of pulling over. To make matters worse there were now two cars behind him, and in his rear-view mirror he could see the impatient look of the motorist following him.

Harris was a confident driver and under different circumstances he would have probably overtaken by now, but today things were very different. There was something holding him back, a heightened awareness perhaps of his own mortality.

The driver behind hooted his horn.

'Okay! Okay!' Harris veered out further. The road ahead looked clear but he would have to be quick, for there was a curve to the right coming up. Shifting gears, he decided to take his chance. He pulled out and sped forward.

Spraying a cloud of leaves and twigs and screeching like an operating sawmill, the hedge-trimming vehicle lumbered out of a concealed farmyard entrance on his right. The huge mechanical arm of the machine swung into view before his windscreen. A lethal blur of rotating, scything blades flashed before him. A blast of car horns erupted in his ears.

At the last moment Harris managed to swing the car over, narrowly avoiding a gruesome death. His heart was thumping wildly as he fought to control his vehicle. For a split second he saw himself lying diced and mangled, his body lacerated beyond recognition; his car windscreen smashed to pieces, the vehicle a sundered wreck.

Then, the danger over, he stepped on the accelerator and sped off, unaware that he was holding his breath until it hurt in his lungs. He heard it gasp harshly as he released it suddenly. There was a peculiar salty taste in his mouth where a thin trickle of blood was flowing from his bitten lower lip.

This was proving to be the worst day of his life, but there was worse to come. Much worse.

★ ★ ★

On the drive back, Harris had decided to call in at home first, to inform his wife of his altered plans.

But she's being questioned by the police over your brutal murder, muttered an insidious little voice inside him.

Fiercely shaking his head, he pulled into his drive and parked the car. Everything was just as he had left it little under an hour ago. There were no policemen stood outside; no crime scene investigators sealing the place off with their lengths of tape.

Nerves tingling, he got out and went up to the front door. With a shaking hand, he removed his key from a pocket, opened the door and went inside. There was no sign of his wife or son, which was of no real surprise, for today was the day they went to her sister's on the other side of town. They would be well on their way there by now.

Taking off his jacket, Harris closed the door behind him and went into the lounge. The domestic normality and familiarity of his surroundings were doing wonders in restoring his peace of mind. He switched on the television, sat on the sofa and waited for the local news to come on.

Ten minutes later, having heard no mention of any dismembered corpse having been found in the vicinity, he forced himself to accept that it had all been purely delusional. Of course it had — after all, he was still here with all his limbs intact. Even the marks around his wrists and ankles had all but vanished. There was a residual puffiness and they were tender to the touch, but apart from that they looked more or less normal.

It had just been a bad morning.

Still, Harris thought a stiff drink would

help calm his nerves. He got up from the sofa and paced over to the drinks cabinet. There was an unopened bottle of single malt whiskey which he had been keeping for his birthday, but right now he thought his current need was greater. Unscrewing the lid, he poured himself a generous measure and went back to the sofa.

The first sip was heavenly. He followed with another, the raw liquor pleasantly warming the back of his throat and soothing his nerves. He leaned back and closed his eyes.

'*Aaaaaagggh!*'

A tortured scream burst from his mouth as instant, agonising pain wrenched through his entire body. The whiskey glass fell from his hand onto the carpeted floor as he leapt to his feet like someone who had just been subjected to an immense electric current. The pain was intense yet fleeting, and he knew that had it lasted a moment longer he would surely have passed out, such was its ferocity.

'What's happening to me?' he yelled to the empty room. 'What the hell's happening to me?'

The bizarre rash was coming back to his wrists. He could see it spreading before his very eyes. The pain in his ankles now flared up again. It was as though he had been manacled by a sadistic torturer who was taking great delight in tightening his leg irons. Invisibly fettered, he somehow staggered into the hallway, the pain biting deeper with every stumble. Frantically, he reached the phone and managed to call for an ambulance. He had just finished when the pain became a dark, blinding sheet of fire that tore through his body, rendering him unconscious.

* * *

Harris's return to consciousness was slow and forced. The sensation was more than a little alarming as his mind, stimulated in part by the mental images carried over from that truly terrible nightmare, conjured up a myriad of dark, unanswered questions. There was a swirling fog inside his brain and his eyes ached. He was lying in a bed that was screened off. Disorientated and unsure of his surroundings, he panicked for a moment, then sat up.

'Help! Will someone tell me where the hell I am?'

A male nurse parted the curtains and peered in. 'Ah, Mr. Harris. I'll go and let the doctor know that you're awake.' He disappeared as quickly as he had appeared.

Stifling the cry that threatened to burst from his lips, Harris freed his arms from the blanket, horrified to see that both wrists now had crude bracelets made of rope wrapped around them.

The curtain was pulled back on its rail and a tall, bespectacled doctor stepped into view. 'Good afternoon, Mr. Harris. I'm Doctor Andrews and I'm pleased to see that you're finally awake.'

Pitifully, Harris held out his arms. 'Help me,' he whimpered. 'For the love of God, help me! Take these things off!'

Doctor Andrews walked forward uncertainly. 'What things?'

'These ropes! They burn and I can feel them tugging at me.'

'But there are no ropes.'

'The pain. Make the pain go away.

217

Please, I'm begging you!'

'Mr. Harris. Having been in touch with your treating psychiatrist, Doctor Yates, I'm of the view that the pain you claim to be experiencing is purely psychosomatic.' Doctor Andrews briefly consulted a medical clipboard. 'You've been X-rayed and thoroughly examined and I'm pleased to say there are absolutely no signs of trauma to either your arms or your legs. I can also assure you that there are no ropes. Now — '

'Does . . . does my wife know I'm here?'

'Yes. I believe she should be along soon, but in the meantime may I suggest that you get some rest.'

'I need painkillers! Give me the strongest you've got. Morphine, something like that.'

'I'm afraid not.' Doctor Andrews shook his head. 'I don't want to prescribe a strong dose of analgesics until we can really assess the true problem here. If indeed there is one at all.' He looked sceptical. After all, there was no evidence to support his patient's claims. Quite the opposite in fact.

'Doctor, I woke this morning having seen my body torn limb from limb! Then something hauled me off the ground and, believe me, I'm definitely in need of painkillers. So don't you stand there and tell me there's no problem.'

'I'm sorry, Mr. Harris. Now if you'll just — '

'To hell with this!' Harris swung his legs out of the bed and got to his feet.

'Please, calm down and — '

'No! I've had enough of this! If I am cracking up then I want to see Doctor Yates.' Harris fought to regain control of his limbs. With difficulty, he managed to hobble his way down the ward, heading for the exit doors. They opened and he saw his wife. 'Pauline,' he called. 'Help me get out of here! Help me get these ropes off!'

There was a grave look on Pauline's face as she rushed to assist her troubled husband.

Ignoring Doctor Andrews's pleas, they both headed out of the hospital.

★ ★ ★

There was an excruciating agony in Harris's extremities as his wife drove down the high street, searching for somewhere convenient to park. He felt like screaming as he watched the bindings on his wrists constrict, crushing the delicate bones under the skin and cutting off the circulation to his hands. His fingers were turning blue. There was a wrenching in his shoulders, and such was the severity that he expected he was going to be torn limb from limb at any moment. The rending pain in his ankles was just as severe.

It was how he imagined an unfortunate being racked would feel. That was it! He was being subjected to some form of mediaeval torture.

Gonzalo Barabas!

The name flashed through his mind. He felt himself slipping in and out of consciousness. A dark hold came over him as the all-out agony tore through his body. The last sight he witnessed before passing out once more was of a fat, jolly-looking butcher chopping meat in a high street shop, his cleaver coming down heavily, separating the cuts of beef.

Out of the darkness shone a pencil-thin beam of intense white light. 'Hello! Is there anybody in there?'

Harris could feel pressure on his right eyelid. He was lying flat on a low couch.

'Mr. Harris. Can you hear me? This is Doctor Yates.' The words were soft and mellow, pleasing on the ear. 'I'm going to give you an injection. You'll feel a little scratch.'

Harris mumbled something. He felt his shirt sleeve being rolled up and then the fleeting stabbing sensation as the hypodermic pierced his skin. Thankfully, it was the only pain that registered at the moment. He felt some of his energy returning and a few minutes later he sat up, noting immediately that the ropes and marks on his arms had vanished.

'I must say you're looking better than you did ten minutes ago.'

'Where's Pauline?' asked Harris, looking around.

'Your wife's gone to collect your son from her sister's, but all I want you to do

221

at the moment is relax.' The psychiatrist returned to his desk. 'I know that we've been over this several times before, but I really think if we want to treat what's plaguing you we'd better go over it once more. So, these nightmares you've been having. When did they first begin?' He sat on the edge of a chair, a pad resting lightly on his right knee. He held a pen poised above it expectantly.

Harris stared vacantly at the ceiling for a long moment, then licked his lips. 'Several weeks ago.'

Doctor Yates nodded and jotted something down on his pad. He eyed his patient observantly. 'I see that you're constantly examining your arms. Your wife mentioned something about ropes.'

'There were ropes fastened around my wrists.'

'And . . . these ropes. I take it they're no longer there?'

'They've gone . . . for the moment. As has the pain.'

'Good.' Doctor Yates eased his tall body into a more comfortable position. 'I take it the pain is always associated with your seeing of the ropes?'

'Not at first, but it seems to be now.'

'And this, shall we say, physical dimension to your dreams has only come on today? No indications of this before?'

'Just this morning. It first happened when I got to work. I was lifted off the ground.'

The psychiatrist's eyebrows raised. 'Interesting.' He scribbled something else on his pad.

'Well what is it, doctor? Am I mad? I guess I must be.'

'Of course not. However, with your permission, I'd like to perform a little experiment. It's quite simple really, but it should give me an insight into your mental processes.'

Harris smiled weakly. 'What sort of experiment, doctor?'

'Nothing elaborate. Merely an association of words. I'm going to say a word and all I want you to do is tell me the first word that you think of. Whether or not it seems to make sense at the time is of little consequence. Are you ready?'

'Yes.

'Very well. Here's the first word: day.'

'Night.'

'Good.'

'Eee . . . evil.'

'Life.'

'Mmm . . . *muerte*.' Harris struggled as the Spanish word for death blurted from his mouth.

Yates sat up. 'White.'

'Nnnn . . . *negro*.'

'Fear.'

'Mmm . . . *miedo, miedo* . . . what's happening?' Harris exclaimed. 'I don't know that word!'

'Try to relax, just say whatever comes to mind.' Yates spoke calmly. 'Torture.'

'*Para! Para por el amor de dios!*' Harris suddenly shrieked. The room seemed to be melting and swirling in front of his eyes, and the tightness was beginning in his wrists and ankles once more.

'You're safe, Anthony. Nothing is happening to you here in my office,' Doctor Yates insisted gently, his voice level and with little variation in tone. 'You need to speak in English. Your native tongue is English, not Spanish. Tell me

224

what you are feeling.'

Harris fought to make his eyes focus but he felt as if he was falling sideways, that the room was tipping. He could feel an intense heat and heard the sound of many people close by. The ropes were back on him and he felt himself lift off the ground, on his back. There was red, rocky sand beneath him. Sweat stung his eyes and there was blazing sunlight on his face.

Terrified, he thrashed his body from side to side and started shouting: 'Anthony Harris! I'm Anthony Harris! *Me llamo Gonzalo Barabas!*' He was vaguely aware that the psychiatrist was bending over him and pulling his head round.

'Look at me, Anthony! You are here, in Croydon. It's March the twenty-ninth, 1972. Look at me!'

Harris gradually felt the sand beneath him turn to carpet. The heat faded and the pain subsided. He was lying spread-eagled on the floor of the psychiatrist's office and sweat was prickling all over his body. He tried to speak but found he was terrified at what might come out of his mouth. Painfully, he pulled himself up into a sitting position.

Doctor Yates brought him a glass of water. 'Drink this and listen . . . no, don't talk for a minute, just listen.' He brought his chair over, opposite Harris. 'I believe that we are finally getting somewhere. Your speech just now, your panic as if you were in mortal danger . . . it all points to one thing — you are remembering a past life; or perhaps I should more accurately say, a past death.'

Harris stared at the man in confusion.

'Many people, many religions, believe that the human soul is reincarnated and lives through many different lifetimes before achieving peace. Normally, the soul has no memory of the other lives, but I have heard of cases where the barrier between one life and the next becomes weak, especially if the individual in question suffered a very traumatic death. People start to have glimpses of other lives they have lived, and this can bring huge problems with it.'

Harris had to say something. 'You can't

really believe that, surely? It's nonsense — religious claptrap!'

'How can you be so sure?' Doctor Yates countered. 'I, too, was sceptical when I first heard about this concept, but I've seen too many patients over the years who have had no basis for their neuroses and aberrations that can be pinpointed in their past. At least, not in their current lives. I've done my best to give them coping strategies but I've never felt satisfied. You, however . . . ' He looked more animated than Harris had ever seen him. 'You may actually be able to access the memories of your former life; and if so, can move past the trauma you experienced. The fact that you are experiencing such a strong manifestation of it shows that it needs to be acknowledged. If you do not, then it will continue to torment you.'

'But this is ridiculous, impossible!' Harris protested, wiping sweat from his face.

'What was your name?' Doctor Yates suddenly demanded, grabbing Harris by the wrists and squeezing hard.

Harris gasped at the pain. 'My name? You know my name. I'm . . . I'm . . . ' He was struggling to shape the words in his mouth. There was an inner conflict taking place, a battle of wills. Inside his head he heard a chorus of voices screeching and shouting in Spanish, their words unintelligible.

Doctor Yates steered his patient back to the couch, where he sat him down. He began waving his pen torch from side to side. 'Focus on the light and answer my questions. Who are you?'

There was a vacant look in Harris's eyes as he began to talk. 'I'm Anthony Brian Harris.'

'Where were you born and in what year?'

'Retford, Nottinghamshire. 1926.'

'What date?'

'April the twelfth.'

'Who were your parents?'

'Jack and Betty Harris.'

Doctor Yates was swinging the light faster. Back and forth. Back and forth. 'You're feeling very sleepy, Anthony. Close your eyes and let your mind drift.

Imagine you're falling down a long, dark tunnel, spiralling away. Down. Down. I'm going to take you back to a time before you were born.'

★ ★ ★

Spitting and cursing, Gonzalo Barabas — thief, bandit, murderer and rapist — was frogmarched through the jeering mob of spectators out into the dusty arena of the converted bullring. The noonday sun was like a furnace that struck at him without mercy, pulsing down at him in great waves of heat, burning and stinging his shirtless, freshly lashed back. With each step, the sand beneath the soles of his bare feet grew hotter. Blood from a rifle-butt wound — a farewell present from one of his gaolers — trickled down the side of his rugged, unshaven face. Like a stream in a gulch, it dribbled down a furrow in his cheek, collecting on a swollen, split bottom lip. His tongue tasted it, relishing the moisture, no matter its source.

The horses were waiting; four large,

powerful creatures that champed and neighed, their flanks flecked with sweat. Stout wooden yokes were being fastened to them by two uniformed men.

There was no time for fear. Fear was for the weak.

Defiantly, Barabas, his face scarred, cracked, bruised and blistered, gazed up at the fiery disc in the sky, the intense brightness burning his piercing green eyes. For a moment he managed to discern its shimmering outline. Then he was roughly pushed forward. He fell to his knees before being hauled upright by the hair.

Half a dozen steps, and then he was manhandled to the ground. The sand burned his back.

Someone was screaming, and it was only after his hands had been securely strapped to the metal bars attached to the lengths of thick rope that he realised it was him. Frantically, he kicked out, landing a scuffing blow on one of his captors. Then his feet were being clamped and bound, as were his hands. Out of the corner of his eye he could see the array of

230

butchering tools spread out on the ground: knives and hatchets — bladed implements that would be called for if the horses failed to . . .

There was a blinding flare of agony as his body was lifted from the sand, raised by the sudden movement of the horses. Then the beasts were being whipped and the true pain began.

★　★　★

Harris screamed and sprang upright. His eyes were staring wildly and sweat boiled from his face. There was a dryness in his throat and he found it hard to swallow.

Doctor Yates had stopped the pendulum-like motion of his pen torch. 'Are you all right, Anthony?' he asked.

'What happened?' Harris gasped.

'Under hypnosis I successfully regressed you to a past life. You were living the last moments of a previous existence. From what I could make out it would appear that you were once a notorious Spanish criminal named Gonzalo Barabas who was sentenced to death sometime in the late seventeenth century. The method of your execution was quartering by wild horses.'

Harris got to his feet. 'No! This can't be happening.'

'You can't hide from your past, Anthony, no matter how much you may want to. It's all embedded here, in your brain,' said Doctor Yates, tapping his temple. 'You were, and to some extent still are, Gonzalo Barabas.'

'No! This is madness!' Harris made for the door. 'Complete and utter — '

'Don't fight it, Anthony. Better to accept and work through the memories.'

'Never!' Harris flung the door wide and lurched out into the waiting room. 'You're the one who's mad! You're the one who needs a doctor!' he shouted over his shoulder. His mind was reeling and his heart was palpitating furiously in his chest. His whole being fizzed and hummed with fear and disbelief, unable and unwilling to accept what his psychiatrist had just told him. Crashing against a door, he stumbled out into the main street.

A man walking his dog cursed as he was bumped into.

Oblivious to the strange looks he was getting, Harris staggered up the street.

You were, and to some extent still are, Gonzalo Barabas. The words preyed on his mind, fastening leech-like to his brain. With each hurried step, he could feel them gnawing away at him, the psychological pain now becoming physical once more as the sense of fugue — of separation from his own self — grew greater.

'Hello. Are you all right?'

A face he thought he knew swam into vision before his eyes.

'You're not looking too good.'

His left leg buckled beneath him and he half-fell into the road, an outstretched hand reaching for the bonnet of a parked car in order to support him.

'You're not drunk, are you? Come on, pull yourself together, man.'

Pull himself together — something was trying to pull him apart! Unsteadily, he edged back on to the pavement.

You were, and to some extent still are, Gonzalo Barabas.

With a cry of utter horror and pain,

Harris was dragged over the car bonnet. There came a terrible ripping sound and, accompanied by a thick jet of blood, his left arm was wrenched from his body.

People screamed as the limb was sent flying across the road.

The gentleman in the now blood-spattered suit who had tried to help Harris stared, wide-eyed and horror-stricken.

His yelling and screaming drowning out that of the horrified bystanders, Harris was now suspended in the middle of the road, his back horribly curved. He was beginning to unravel. There came a further tearing noise as the bones and sinews of his right arm were stretched to breaking point. Then, with a pop and a wet-sounding splatter, the limb was ruptured, torn from its socket. It went spiralling into the air, hit a shop window and, leaving a messy smear down the glass, landed on the ground, whereupon a dog quickly snatched it up and ran off with it.

His arms having now been reduced to unsightly stumps of bone, blood and gristle, what remained of Harris was dragged by unseen forces down the centre of the road. Still very much alive, he felt every moment of excruciating agony as first one leg, then the other, was torn from his body.

And then a darkness began to descend.

There were people standing over him, looking down in fearful, morbid curiosity. In the distance he thought he could hear the sound of an approaching siren.

'Jesus Christ! I've never seen anything like it.'

'Poor bastard! His eyes are still moving!'

'Anybody know who he is?'

It was just as death finally took him that he heard the last voice.

'His name is Gonzalo Barabas. He is — or rather was — a wanted man in Spain.' Doctor Yates looked down indifferently on the messy remains of his patient, wondering if he had finally perfected his method of murdering by past-life regression and psychological suggestion — and the occasional surreptitiously administered drug. There were a few more test subjects he was working on;

but this trial, as he considered it, had proved demonstrably successful. Smiling to himself with satisfaction, he turned and walked away.

We do hope that you have enjoyed reading this large print book.

Did you know that all of our titles are available for purchase?

We publish a wide range of high quality large print books including:
Romances, Mysteries, Classics
General Fiction
Non Fiction and Westerns

Special interest titles available in large print are:
The Little Oxford Dictionary
Music Book, Song Book
Hymn Book, Service Book

Also available from us courtesy of Oxford University Press:
Young Readers' Dictionary
(large print edition)
Young Readers' Thesaurus
(large print edition)

For further information or a free brochure, please contact us at:
Ulverscroft Large Print Books Ltd.,
The Green, Bradgate Road, Anstey,
Leicester, LE7 7FU, England.
Tel: (00 44) 0116 236 4325
Fax: (00 44) 0116 234 0205

HOLLYWOOD HEAT

Arlette Lees

1950s Los Angeles: When six-year-old Daisy Adler vanishes from her upscale Hollywood Hills home, Detective Rusty Hallinan enters a case with more dangerous twists and turns than Mulholland Drive. Hallinan's life hits a bump or two of its own when he's dumped by his wife and falls for an enchanting young murder suspect half his age. But what's the connection between her murdered husband and a dying bar-room stripper? How does Hallinan's informant, exotic and endangered female impersonator Tyrisse Covington, fit into the puzzle? And where has little Daisy gone?

THE WITCHES' MOON

Gerald Verner

Mr. Dench left his house on a wet September night to post a letter at a nearby pillar-box — and disappeared. A fortnight later his dead body was found in a tunnel a few miles away. He had been brutally murdered. Called in to investigate, Superintendent Robert Budd soon realizes that Dench hadn't planned to disappear. But it's not until he finds the secret of the fireman's helmet, the poetic pickpocket, and the Witches' Moon that he discovers why Mr. Dench — and several other people — have been murdered . . .

TILL THE DAY DAY I DIE

V. J. Banis

Shot at point-blank range while trying to prevent the kidnapping of her daughter Becky, book editor Catherine Desmond has a mysterious near-death experience. When she recovers, she learns that Becky has been murdered by a gang of child abusers, who are still active and being hunted by the police. To her dismay, she finds herself linked psychically with Becky's killer — and he begins shadowing her as well. An ethereal cat-and-mouse game ensues, with life — and death — hanging in the balance . . .